IMELDA'S SECRET

LIZA GINO

IMELDA
Torn Image

Imelda's Secret

LIZA GINO

To Joe,

May this inspire
and empower you!

[signature]
10-2022

Published By
Liza Gino

ISBN 978-1-7358070-0-3 (paperback)
ISBN 978-1-7358070-1-0 (kindle ebook)
Library of Congress Control Number: 2020919303

Published by
Liza Gino
www.ImeldasSecret.com

DEDICATED TO
MY ANGELS:
DADDY, GINNY, & OYET

TABLE OF CONTENTS

TABLE OF IMAGES

PRAYER FOR HEALING VICTIMS OF ABUSE

PASTOR ROZITA VILLANUEVA LEE

Our Heavenly Father, we come before you humbly and praise you for your love and thank you for the breath of life as we serve your purpose in your kingdom on earth.

Father, we remember today the thousands of women who endured humiliation and shame during World War II at the hands of the Japanese soldiers.

They suffered not in the battlefield bombarded with guns and bombs but in ways much worse. These women, many of them in their early teens, were kidnapped from their home countries by the Japanese and transported to other countries where they were abused and raped and were forced into servitude as "comfort women."

Dear God, many of these women did not survive the atrocity and succumbed to diseases and illnesses contracted from the Japanese but those who survived were never the same.

After the war, some survivors were repatriated to their respective countries while others, overcome with shame, decided to live out the rest of their lives away from their families. In 2020, only a handful of these women remain alive but are constantly struggling with traumatic nightmares and illnesses and questions of why. They are asking why Japan has not apologized to them and to their respective countries. Why have no reparations been made for the abuse they suffered?

Father, we do not know if Japan will ever apologize but we ask that you be with the organizations that are supporting these women in their quest for an apology and reparation. Give them the wisdom and understanding to handle this situation. Open up the heart of the Emperor and the present leadership of Japan.

But most of all, dear Lord, we pray for the survivors and their families and ask that you blanket them with your healing love. We place all involved in your hands and pray that justice be served.

For we pray this in the name of the Father, the Son, and the Holy Spirit.

AMEN!

PREFACE

JUDITH MIRKINSON

President, "Comfort Women" Justice Coalition

The underlying history behind this novel is true. It did happen.

From 1931 to 1945, during the Pacific War, the Imperial Japanese Army created and implemented the largest institutionalized system of sexual slavery in the 20th century.

The first so-called "comfort station" was established in Shanghai, China but they soon spread throughout Asia. Some were actual brothels in houses, others were just in caves or sheds, some were even on the front lines.

Hundreds of thousands of young women and girls (the average age was 15-16, but there were girls as young as 11) were kidnapped and coerced to "sexually service" Japanese military personnel. They were euphemistically called "comfort women." It's estimated that as many as 400,000 were abducted. The majority were from China and Korea but young women and girls were also taken from every country Japan occupied, including the Philippines, Malaysia, Indonesia, Taiwan, and Hong Kong. The women were held at gunpoint and raped repeatedly, sometimes as many as 40 times a day!

The majority of the women died from the constant abuse. The 10 percent that survived remained silent for nearly 40 years until 1991 when Hak Soon Kim, a former "comfort woman" from Korea, spoke out publicly for the first time. Hundreds of others soon joined her.

Just as their Korean sisters were stigmatized, thus preventing them to speak out sooner, "comfort women" survivors in the Philippines also kept their silence. But emboldened by the testimony in Korea they, too, began to speak out. The rumors about what had happened had been there for decades. Women recall their grandmothers sharing stories of their mothers hiding them in basements and large vats of rice. The tale of Imelda and Gloria being dressed up as boys echoes what happened in real life.

In 1992, Maria Rosa Henson, or Nana Rosa, became the first Filipino woman to tell her story. Many followed her example. They did so in the face of and in spite of frequent and uncomfortable public scrutiny and even shaming from their own families. The women formed a group called Lila Pilipina, which is still active today, in order to obtain recognition and justice from Japan for those who had been sexually enslaved.

RAPE AND SEXUAL SLAVERY AS A WAR CRIME AND CRIME AGAINST HUMANITY

Although long outlawed under international law, rape during wartime has always been viewed as normal. It is euphemistically referred to as "spoils of war" and dismissed as just "the way it is." When the "comfort women" survivors began to speak out, they did so within the context of a growing recognition that rape during wars was something that

6

should not be tolerated. The wars in Yugoslavia and Rwanda highlighted the horrific use of rape and sexual slavery as a strategy of ethnic cleansing and domination. The experiences of the "comfort women" were very much in people's minds when, in1993, the Vienna Declaration of the World Conference of Human Rights named rape as a form of torture. In 1998, the international community ratified the Rome Statute, which classified rape and sexual slavery as a strategy of war as a war crime. In 2008 the U.N. Security Council adopted resolution 1820, which noted that "rape and other forms of sexual violence can constitute war crimes, crimes against humanity or a constitutive act with respect to genocide." Women can now speak about what was once regarded as unspeakable. The willingness to address openly the issue of systematic rape owes a great deal to the courage of former "comfort women" and women from Bosnia, Rwanda, and Congo.

Does this mean that women are no longer raped in instances of armed conflict or that sexual servitude is no longer a feature of colonial domination? Of course not. Culture does not change overnight as history tells us. We can see that today in the treatment of women in Syria, Kashmir and Myanmar. But the fact that the international community acknowledges that it should be stopped does matter a great deal. It gives us a basis from which to continue the fight. The shame women feel upon being raped is slowly beginning to dissipate. In 2018, Nadia Murad, a young Yazidi woman from Iraq, was awarded the Nobel Peace Prize for speaking out about having been sexually enslaved by ISIS.

The testimony of the "comfort women" helped humanize the issue and was significant in changing human perception and behavior towards sexual abuse.

The Imperial Japanese Army's systematic practice of sexual slavery had other far-reaching implications. Although most of the kidnapped young women were imprisoned relatively close to their homes, a significant number were trafficked to other countries. Korean women were sent to China, Chinese women ended up in Burma. In essence, this was the beginning of government-sponsored sex trafficking.

JAPAN MUST APOLOGIZE

Despite overwhelming evidence, the Japanese government still will not give an official apology through the Diet (their governing body) to the survivors and their families. In fact, over the past few years, they have done everything to deny the atrocities the women suffered decades ago. The topic of "comfort women" has been taken out of Japanese text books and Japanese officials even tried to get a US textbook publisher do the same. Any attempt to memorialize these brave women has been met with fierce Japanese resistance.

A perfect example is the case of the Filipina Comfort Women, a statue publicly displayed along Baywalk Roxas Boulevard in Manila, Philippines. It was unveiled on December 8, 2017 and installed through the National Historical Commission of the Philippines (NHCP) and other donors and foundations. However, on April 27, 2018, it was unceremoniously removed in the middle of the night under the cover of darkness. The government claimed that the removal was necessary for road improvements but supporters know this as falsehood. It's clear that the Philippine government was pressured to take down the statue as subsequent efforts was met with similar resistance.

It is common knowledge that Japan tried to pressure other countries to either remove or block installations of similar memorials. The Japanese government is often successful as it wields a lot of power internationally, but sometimes they are not. In 2018, the city of Osaka, Japan broke a 60-year-old sister city relationship with the city of San Francisco, CA over the installation of a "comfort women" memorial statue. The proudly independent American city refused to give in and the "Comfort Women: Column of Strength" memorial stands tall in a beautiful park inside St. Mary's Square.

We Will Not Forget You

There are several dozen "comfort women" surviving in the world today with only a handful living in the Philippines. They are aging and many are sick. Perhaps this is one part of Japan's strategy: to let all the women die and the issue die with them?

But the women and their supporters refuse to give up.

The demands of the movement are clear:

1.   Acknowledge the war crime.

2.   Reveal the truth in its entirety about the crimes of military sexual slavery.

3.   Make an official apology by the Japanese Government.

4.   Make legal reparations.

5.   Punish those responsible for the war crime.

6.   Accurately record the crime in history textbooks.

7.   Erect a memorial for the victims of military sexual slavery and establish a historical museum.

"Imelda's Secret" adds to our collective memory of what happened, as such, it becomes part of the fight to make gender violence and sexual slavery a thing of the past. But to make this real will require commitment and continuing struggle. We must demand accountability and real change.

As women in Lila Filipina put it:

"As women, what we are asking for is justice, for it to be admitted to us, to the whole world, that the Japanese government committed atrocities on us.. All we are asking for is justice!"

FOREWORD

MIHO KIM

Cofounder, "Comfort Women" Justice Coalition

The story of Imelda and Gloria, the two protagonists of this book, is being presented at a time when, just like their own stories, silenced voices from the past are crying out for justice. From #MeToo to Black Lives Matter, the voices of an immeasurable number of faceless victims are calling from the past to demand it so that they may once and for all rest in peace. It is through our beating hearts, as vessels, that these victims will have a chance to redeem their honor and ensure that they shall never be forgotten. As such, our job is to put all of ourselves – mind, body and spirit – to work in the service of this sacred unfinished mission until our hearts give up and we join them in the spirit world.

In the case of the "comfort women," the Imperial Japanese Army "procured" the defenseless poor young women as part of military supply orders along with toilet papers, stationery, and the like, throughout the Asia Pacific region. To think even for a moment that a human being can be reduced to a garbage receptacle for the fleeting release of countless soldiers either crazed or delirious, or both, from their constant dance with death in the sweltering heat, oceans away from home, is to imagine the unimaginable of all nightmares. To see the victims raise their feeble voices and trembling fists to demand justice for seven decades now – whether they are from China, Korea, East Timor, the Philippines or elsewhere – is to bear witness to these women's undeniable fortitude and universal quest for human dignity. There is a need, therefore, for a world order based on the sanctity of all people's most fundamental right to a life with dignity.

Imelda and Gloria may exist in fiction, but they give names to the nameless women who perished into the dark abyss of oblivion, most definitely cold, terrified, hungry and alone. Their life journeys reveal the whole person behind the closed quotes or statistics of "comfort women" or the sterilized portrayal of the "helpless victim" that beg for charity and rescue. We get to feel their feels, relate to their pain, and share in their joy. Above all, we draw power from their resilience and agency. They are perfectly imperfect human beings, damaged goods like the rest of us, making choices that invariably hurt others, and like us, they also come to regret. They also etched indelible marks of their brave acts of love in the hearts of their loved ones. From this close-up intimate journey with Imelda and Gloria, we are able to identify with the "comfort women" from sister to sister, victim to ally, survivor to comrade; defying time and space, transcending all boundaries.

The story of these women helps us put the voices of the survivors and their plea for justice front and center of our work. During the civil rights movement, many African American organizers in the South refused to be silenced based on the belief that "if you don't tell your own stories, someone else will tell it for you." And history shows us time and again, that when others tell our stories, it is neither faithful nor respectful of the truth. The Japanese military never had the right to rob the young women of their birthright to be seen and heard on their terms. Imelda steps into her power as she declares that she will reveal the truth. Her resolve is contagious. By the time we put the book down, we shall find, in Liza's own words, "the fire in our bellies," that will propel us to "rise up and unite across and above (and in spite of) all borders and boundaries that divide, categorize and label us apart from each other, and incite collective action."

Their story is also our story. Their fight is a universal issue, in the here and now, no matter where. After all, the Universal Declaration of Human Rights, a landmark document in the history of human rights, opens with this declaration: "Recognition of the inherent dignity and of the equal and inalienable rights of all members of the human family is the foundation of freedom, justice and peace in the world."

It is not important that the horrific history of Japanese military sexual slavery system occurred decades ago, in fact, "[t]his is not an issue relegated to history," as the United Nations High Commissioner for Human Rights, Navi Pillay, has stressed. "It is a current issue, as human rights violations against these women continue to occur, as long as their rights to justice and reparation are not realized."

So let us all unite urgently. Let us elevate the voices of the victims and end this egregious human rights violation by fulfilling their inalienable rights so we can strengthen the foundation of justice for all of our future girls and women around the world.

"VISIONS"

JEANNIE E. CELESTIAL, PHD, LCSW

Mental Health Resources

Trigger Warning & Self-Care Invitation: *This resource guide contains words and concepts that may evoke strong emotions and bodily sensations. Please read it in a safe place and ground yourself back in your body especially if operating machinery or driving a vehicle afterwards. Remember to breathe and be compassionate with yourself while reading.*

One of the toughest aspects of secrets is their weight. Secrets can be heavy burdens that people may carry around for years, decades, or even a lifetime. Secrets can keep people locked in an invisible prison of shame and silence. Secrets separate us from parts of ourselves, others, and community. In Imelda's case, keeping her secret from even her closest family members was a manifestation of trauma—experiencing and witnessing life-threatening physical, emotional, and sexual violence.

Imelda's Secret brings us into the hearts and minds of Imelda, Gloria, and other survivors of trauma. In most cultures, this topic is difficult to talk about. Survivors may keep their abuse secret from the people around them for self-preservation and survival. This book invites all abuse survivors to acknowledge and honor their pain and have courage to seek support and healing. This book encourages survivors to voice what was believed to be unspeakable. *Imelda's Secret* beckons survivors to reclaim their bodies and minds and to find healing and integration.

This book sheds light on the lasting effects of trauma on the minds, bodies, and spirits of survivors. Traumatic memories may intrude survivors' thoughts and sleep, inhibiting a sense of inner peace. Survivors may avoid people, places, or things that remind them of the trauma. They may develop and carry negative beliefs about themselves related to shame, unworthiness, or being tarnished or no longer lovable. Survivors may also suffer from persistent mood changes, such as sadness or irritability, and/or lose interest in things they used to enjoy. Survivors may live in a constant state of high alert, scanning the environment for danger.

If you or someone you love is a survivor of abuse, you are not alone. The abuse you experienced was not your fault. Your feelings are valid. You have inherent value as you are. You are worthy of love and of giving love.

If you or someone you love is a survivor of abuse, help is available. While trauma may have led you to struggle alone, there are people who can support you. Please reach out to a trusted friend, family member, spiritual guide, and/or professional advocate or counselor. Please find a trusted person or group to hold space for the traumatic experience/s that may have felt intolerable for so long.

If you are a descendent or family member of an abuse survivor, you may be impacted by intergenerational trauma—the effects of trauma that can get passed down from one generation to the next. Intergenerational trauma can take the form of unhealthy patterns of mood or behavior, such as family violence or substance abuse, or negative beliefs about oneself, others, or the world. If you believe you may suffer from the intergenerational trauma, you, too, may benefit from support and help.

Imelda and Gloria's stories did not end with the abuse. They survived, persisted, and lived resilient lives. They grew and transformed their trauma as they were able. It is our hope that survivors reading this book will also find recovery and wholeness.

Self-Care for the Reader:

The stories in this book depict violence and torture. It may be useful to examine how you as the reader may be impacted by the book's content in body, mind, and spirit. After reading this book, you might find it helpful to engage your senses with soothing activities, such as: coloring a pattern with crayons or markers, taking a walk or dancing, cooking, praying or meditating, drawing, journaling, writing a poem, smelling something comforting (e.g., lavender or mint), drinking water or herbal tea, listening to music, eating a healthy snack, petting a dog or cat, hugging a friend or family member, and/or taking a warm bath. Tune in to what you need, and take care of yourself.

Resources:
National Sexual Assault Hotline (USA)
https://www.rainn.org/

1-800-656-HOPE (4673)

National Domestic Violence Hotline (USA)
https://www.thehotline.org/
1-800-799-SAFE (7233)
TTY: 1-800-787-3224

National Human Trafficking Hotline
https://humantraffickinghotline.org/
1-888-373-7888
TTY: 711

Text: 233733

National Human Trafficking Resource Center Hotline
http://www.endslaverynow.org/act/report-a-tip
1-888-373-7888

Comfort Women Justice Coalition
https://remembercomfortwomen.org

How to take a stand against the culture of rape
https://www.unwomen.org/en/news/stories/2019/11/compilation-ways-you-can-stand-against-rape-culture

Violence Against Women Hotlines (Philippines)
https://www.lguvscovid.ph/content/violence-against-women-hotlines
PNP Hotline: 177

Aleng Pulis Hotline: (+63)919 777 7377

Philippine Commission on Women
https://pcw.gov.ph/

ACKNOWLEDGEMENT

I would like to start off by thanking you, the reader, for picking up this book. As you read this book, I aspire to show you the life of the comfort women. I hope that after you finish reading, it inspires you to do something. You can be the agent of change. I encourage you to make a change, no matter how small to make things better for all.

To my children: Bianca, Margaux, and Johann, I am forever grateful. I am proud of you and all that you do. I wrote "Imelda's Secret," not just to tell a story but to put out a message to enlighten. You are the reason I keep going. May your path be always illuminated with knowledge.

Thank you to my family and friends for sharing your stories, experiences, and eyewitness accounts. You gave this novel its soul and a reason to provide clarity and purpose. I could not have written this without you, and I pray I did your stories justice. I owe you my gratitude for unveiling the secret.

I am grateful to Pastor Rozita for writing the prayer. It was essential to start with a prayer because this novel is about the abused and the need for healing. In times of need, one tends to look for a higher power to bring relief and understanding. I consider prayer as a form of meditation to contemplate and to garner strength. We pray to find peace.

I am indebted to Judith Mirkinson, President, "Comfort Women" Justice Coalition, who wrote the preface. The importance of bringing an academic and historical perspective cannot be denied. Though this novel was about the Filipina comfort women, there were thousands of women in various nations that suffered the same ordeal. Judith brought the framework to expound on the extent of abuse and unprecedented harm. I am so very thankful for the knowledge you imparted.

To Miho Kim, Cofounder, San Francisco Comfort Women Justice Coalition, who wrote the foreword, I am so grateful for your contribution. Your beautiful words will bring cohesion to this entire book. The preface brought the past and your foreword brought to prominence what can be done for all these women today. As a world leader, especially among women, your words go a long way by inspiring change and inciting action.

My editors: Bianca Andrea Collver, Ana Treñas, and Raymond Lo, did more than help me. Bianca, your work on this novel was more than dotting the i's and crossing the t's. You shared my adventure and your assistance brought depth and flavor at a personal cost. Your support and belief in this project sustained and brought me to completion, for which I am always grateful. Ana and Raymond, your talents and expertise are immeasurable. Thank you all for everything that you have done.

The mental health resources section provides good information that has been carefully put together by Jeannie Celestial, PhD, LCSW.

I am grateful for her input which completes this book in providing pathways to wellness and peace.

Special thanks go to Maria Isabel Lopez and Angeli Clarisse Lata for providing an image of Imelda for the book cover. Angeli's masterful illustration and Isabel's haunting mixed media mosaic artwork give the readers an idea of Imelda's present, past and future self.

And, lastly, to you, my special one. Thank you for everything.

UP IN THE TREES

Imelda steadied herself on the tree limb and reached down to tap Gloria on the shoulder. With tears in her eyes, Gloria looked up at Imelda.

This was not how tonight was supposed to be. In Gloria's mind, their faces and hair were made up and gorgeous, dancing in beautiful gowns. The gentle breeze carried the sounds of music and light banter. Perfume hung in the air from the ladies gliding about on gentlemen's arms. Everything was beautiful. Perfect.

The spark of fired shots caused Imelda and Gloria to cling more tightly to the mango tree. The soldiers were shooting aimlessly into the dark, hoping to hit anyone who may be hiding. The young women preferred getting shot to being captured.

"If Gloria would only listen," Imelda said to herself. "We would have been safe with Papa."

Earlier that night, Gloria had stormed out of the basement. She kept running until she could no longer run, but Gloria was not the athletic type, so she did not get far. Imelda was able to catch up with her easily.

"Enough!" Gloria cried out as she pushed Imelda away.

"We have to get back," Imelda yelled out forcefully. "It will be dark soon. We might run into Japanese soldiers. It is not safe!"

"Who cares?" Gloria answered as she continued walking away from Imelda. "I've had it! I can't stand being cooped up in that basement. It stinks in there!"

"I know, but it is safer there than out here," Imelda said as she pulled on Gloria's arm.

"And look at us, Imelda. This is not us. What are we wearing? I hate wearing trousers! I know you are comfortable, but I don't like it. And why can't we try to make ourselves look pretty, or at least decent?" asked Gloria, pulling on her pant legs.

She looked down at her clothing and her arms covered in dirt and exclaimed, "I want to take a bath. I don't like being smelly or having to roll around in the mud. My arms, legs, and face are all covered in dirt. I even have dirt in my hair, or rather what's left of it."

Gloria put her hands on her head. "I miss my hair!" she blurted out. She shook her head violently, but the short, uneven hair stood up defiantly, stiff with mud from root to tip.

"Gloria, you know why," Imelda answered, putting her arm around her cousin. "You know very well what could happen. We don't want to end up like Clara."

Gloria burst into tears. A year older than Imelda and Gloria,

Clara was adored by men for her beauty. A marriage proposal soon followed her coronation as *Mutya ng Lipa* at the last town fiesta. The impending wedding was anticipated as the most prominent social event the town would ever see, but after two months of intensive planning the Japanese arrived.

Clara lived next door to Imelda and Gloria. Her family was having a dinner party when soldiers stormed into her home, firing shots into the ceiling. Women began to cry and hide behind their men. The men stretched out their arms in a futile attempt to shield them.

Neighboring homes suddenly fell quiet. Lights were extinguished, windows were shut, and doors were locked. The nearby houses stood quietly, witnessing the horror as it unfolded.

Don Fulgencio hurriedly took his daughter Imelda and niece Gloria from their bedrooms and pushed them into a tiny pantry by the back-kitchen, the "*dirty kitchen*". He assumed that no soldier would bother to look where the maids do the rough kitchen work and where all the firewood is stored. He told them to stay silent and still as stone. Don Fulgencio instructed them in a soft but firm voice to remain hidden until he returned for them.

After doing what he could to keep the girls safe, he cautiously crept toward the window to see what was happening next door. He cringed at what he saw.

The Japanese soldiers had pushed everyone out of the house and into the street. Men were sorted from the women, and half of them were shoved up against a wall. The soldiers pushed about half of the men against the wall. The women cried as they clung to their brothers, husbands and sons, but anyone who refused to obey was quickly struck with the butt of a soldier's rifle. One soldier brutally hit a woman in the face. When her husband tried to protest, the soldier silenced him with a stab from his bayonet. Mortally wounded, he fell forward unto her causing her to kneel next to him and start wailing uncontrollably.

The men, lined up against the wall, were shot at point-blank. Don Fulgencio was sickened by what seemed like smiles on the soldiers' faces as they did their duty. Screams of horror punctuated gunshots as bodies fell wounded or dead onto the street. A few soldiers ran to the fallen and stabbed the bodies with their bayonets with perverted pleasure. Don Fulgencio wondered if he could believe what he was seeing. Other soldiers prevented the women from running to their bloodied husbands.

The soldiers gathered those who still lived, herded them with their rifles. They pushed and kicked their captives as they mocked them. Don Fulgencio watched his neighbors cry and try to huddle together as they were marched away. A couple of women were inconsolable as they wailed in agony until the soldiers threatened to hit them. The women covered their mouths struggling to stifle their cries, but they could not help themselves. The sweltering evening air carried their cries as a badge of horror and pain. Even the frogs and crickets crouched in silence, not daring to compete with the torrent of misery.

The following morning, the town was buzzing with trepidation by the news of what happened to the rest of the dinner party. Women who went to the river to do their daily laundry were horrified to find the water red with blood. Scattered along the riverbanks, they found the headless and bloodied bodies of the captives. All who had been taken captive were accounted for, except for Clara and two other women.

A few days later, rumors circulated about a red house where the Japanese conducted their atrocious abuse. Town folks believed that the missing women, including Clara, were at the red house. Screams emanated from the place day and night, and notoriously, women were known to enter the house but never leave alive.

The Japanese came with promises of peace and prosperity, but it was all a lie. If anything, they brought chaos and fear. Homes were torched and the senseless killing gripped the town in terror.

Don Fulgencio did not waste any time after the pillaging started. Since the massacre of his neighbors, he feared for his life and that of his family. Don Fulgencio hurriedly called both Imelda and Gloria into his room. With a big pair of scissors, he took Imelda's hair into his fist and crudely sheared her tresses. He did the same to Gloria. He fought off the tears brimming in his eyes as both girls protested. "Don Fulgencio has gone mad!" they wailed

"*Hijas*, I'm doing this for your own good," Don Fulgencio tried to reassure them.

"Papa, my hair…You took it all off," Imelda moaned, holding onto a lock of her hair.

"*Tio* Fule, are you insane?!" Gloria bellowed, forcefully trying to push his hands away.

Don Fulgencio stared back at Gloria. He had never heard her speak to him in this manner. He would have slapped her, but not today because the world they knew has changed drastically.

"From now on, you will both dress as boys," he commanded. "No more perfume. No more skirts. You will wear the clothing of your *Yaya* Pacing's son."

"But, Papa, why?" asked Imelda in anguish.

"*Tio* Fule, this is madness!" Gloria declared as she looked at the hair strewn about on the floor.

Don Fulgencio hugged both girls. "I'm trying to keep you safe from the Japanese!" he said fearfully.

25

"From now on, we will live in our basement. Hopefully, our *silong* will keep us out of harm's way for now because not many know about this basement. It is no longer safe to stay here," Don Fulgencio explained, looking around the room longingly.

"The basement! It's so small. We use the *silong* for storage and not to live in," Gloria exclaimed.

"I know, *hija*," Don Fulgencio agreed. "Our remaining help and some friends will join us in the *silong*. Others are leaving for Taal Volcano to hide there."

"It will be so crowded," Imelda said, visualizing the *silong* with everyone inside it.

"*Hija*," Don Fulgencio replied. "We have to make room for everyone. We cannot hand them over to the Japanese. That is why you can only take a few things with you. Only those of extreme value. We don't know how long we will have to stay there."

He put a hand on each of their heads and ran his fingers through their now very short hair.

"One day, *hija*, all this madness will end," Don Fulgencio promised.

THE WAY WE WERE

"Honey, wake-up," Ryan said.

Imelda slowly opened her eyes. She blinked several times and fixed her eyeglasses. Ryan was crouched in front of her, gently holding her hand. He smiled faintly as he tugged at her hand.

"You fell asleep, honey. They just brought Gloria back to her room," Ryan told her, motioning to the windows lining the hospital corridor.

Imelda sat up and set the magazine she was reading onto the side table. She quickly ran her fingers through her hair, stood up, gently pulled her sweater down, and straightened her skirt.

She walked to the door and placed her hand on the doorknob. She opened the door of the waiting room and caught a reflection of herself in the glass window. She could not help pausing to look at her reflection.

IMELDA

1980s

Noticing her hair was mostly white now, and her wrinkles more pronounced, "I'm a very old lady," she said to herself with a sigh.

She took a deep breath and walked into Gloria's room.

Imelda gasped, unprepared for what lay before her. Gloria was on the hospital bed with a thin blanket barely covering her. The uncovered areas exposed the intravenous lines and the wires connected to a monitor hanging on the pole next to her bed. With her eyes closed, and her lips parched, Gloria looked serene, yet there was a consistent beeping sound from the machine that controlled the IV drip. Another device that monitored her blood pressure and heart rate emitted constant beeps as well. Seeing the IV and all the wires connected to Gloria was frightening.

Sensing Imelda's presence, Gloria slowly opened her eyes. She could make out a figure but was not sure who stood in the doorway. As she squinted and struggled to see, Imelda rushed to the night table and handed Gloria her eyeglasses.

"Thank you," Gloria whispered as she put on her glasses.

"Ryan and I came as soon as Barry told us," Imelda said, grasping Gloria's hand. She motioned to Ryan, who was still standing by the doorway.

"You know Barry," Gloria said weakly. "He is quite the worrywart. I told him that it was no big deal."

"But it is a big deal," Imelda averred, squeezing Gloria's slender hand. "Barry said you started throwing up and convulsing. We are just so glad that he got you here in time."

"All this fuss for nothing!" Gloria muttered.

"Let's face it, Gloria, you wanted the attention," Ryan said, winking at her. "So, where is Barry, your loving husband?"

"He went to get Bruce," Gloria responded. "I guess Bruce is in trouble again."

Both Imelda and Ryan looked concerned and were about to say something when Gloria spoke first, "Don't worry. Barry didn't actually say anything. I only assumed my wayward son is in trouble again. I'm just glad that Barry tries his best, even if he is not Bruce's father."

"Barry is living proof that the third time's the charm," Ryan said.

Imelda elbowed Ryan. "So, does Kent know? Do you want us to call him?" Imelda asked.

"He knows. He said that he would come by as soon as he drops off Margaux and Johann at school," Gloria explained.

"The twins are so cute!" Imelda blurted. "I imagine that it is quite exhausting when they come to visit you. I should talk to Kent and tell him to limit the time they spend with you."

"You will do no such thing," Gloria declared. "My grandkids make me happy."

"Kids are fun, especially grandkids. You can give them back to their parents anytime." Ryan said with a big grin on his face. "It would be nice if we had one to do the same with, huh?"

"Ryan," said Imelda, "our Adele will have a baby when she is ready."

"Well, she better hurry," answered Ryan. "She will not be young forever."

"Youth!" Gloria mused. "It is a wonderful thing. We were all young once."

"Imelda was particularly spirited," Ryan said, looking at her and putting his arm around her waist – but Imelda shrank away from him.

"I know," confirmed Gloria, managing a faint smile.

Imelda was always an unusually quiet person. Gloria remembered how in their youth, Imelda had always kept to herself and her horses, or her books. Thanks to Gloria's gregarious nature, however, Imelda was not totally lost to her own world of quiet indulgence. Gloria recalled one particular day, decades ago, when Imelda was so excited…

"Come, Gloria, and hurry!" exclaimed Imelda as she burst into Gloria's bedroom.

Gloria immediately sat up in her bed. "What's happening?"

"Ignacio, the groom, told me that there is a new stallion in the stables. I think Papa just got me a new horse! Ignacio said he is beautiful. I have to go see him right away," Imelda said excitedly.

"Huh!?" said Gloria. "And I thought Diego's come back with his cousin Enrique from Bataan."

"What does that have to do with anything?" Imelda wondered as she sat next to Gloria.

"Well, you're always alone at the parties and dances, so we decided to find you a date. Who knows, you might like this one," Gloria explained.

"What!? You did not!" exclaimed Imelda. "Those boys just don't interest me."

"I know," Gloria uttered with disdain. "Just horses and only horses. And books."

"Well, come on," Imelda said, jumping off Gloria's bed. "I really want to see that horse."

"I'm hurrying!" Gloria replied as she dressed.

"I'll meet you in the *sala*," Imelda said excitedly. "Papa is out and about already. *Yaya* Pacing said he is entertaining some foreigners. I think she said they are Americans."

"*Tio* Fule has guests again?" Gloria asked. "I wonder what business he has with these ones."

"I'm sure he will tell us. Now, come on. Hurry!" Imelda shouted from the *sala* just outside of Gloria's bedroom.

Gloria followed reluctantly, but they still arrived at the stables fairly quickly. Imelda was already in her riding breeches. She was not going to waste a moment.

At the stables, there seemed to be some commotion. The stable hands were trying to hold down a horse that was rearing and bucking wildly. Ignacio was holding onto the harness.

Imelda poked into the throng undaunted and reached out for the stallion. She briefly held onto its muzzle. When she reached for the horse again, she cradled its cheek. By the third time Imelda touched the horse, it had calmed down considerably.

"*Señorita*!" exclaimed Ignacio. "Please be careful."

"It's alright, Ignacio," said Imelda as she comforted the horse. "I have this."

Gently, she led the horse into a stall while stroking its neck and whispering into its ear.

"*Señorita*," said Ignacio. "You truly have the gift. The three of us struggled to control Kronos."

"That is a great name for him!" exclaimed Imelda as she examined the horse.

Kronos was a gorgeous Appaloosa stallion. From his muzzle to his withers, Kronos' coat was a deep and beautiful black. The middle of his torso was studded with white spots, and his rump was all white to his tail. Standing proudly at about seventeen hands, he was a very handsome horse.

"I'm going to ride him," Imelda declared.

"I don't think that is a good idea, *Señorita*," Ignacio cautioned. "We just got him, and he seems to be highly spirited. You might not be safe."

"Ignacio, you just told me I have the *gift*. Surely, I can handle him. Give me the tack, and I will put it on him myself," instructed Imelda.

Reluctantly, Ignacio helped Imelda saddle the horse. She worked methodically, putting on the riding bridle and saddle, and Kronos stood calmly. She had one foot on the stirrup when two young Americans briskly closed in on her.

"Now, hold on! What do you think you are doing?" asked the tall blond-haired American.

"I'm going to ride my new horse," Imelda said as she swung into the saddle. "And who are you to ask me such a question?"

"I'm Ryan, and Kronos was my horse," he answered calmly.

"Well, as you said, he was your horse. Now he is mine." Imelda stated. "Now, kindly move aside."

"Now, Missy," Ryan exclaimed, reaching for the reins. "You do not know Kronos like I do. He is much too spirited for you."

"Missy? How much spirit I can or cannot handle is none of your concern. Thank you," Imelda said, with that, she gave Kronos a kick, and the horse bolted out of the stables.

Ryan saw the horse that was saddled up for Gloria. He quickly swung up onto it and chased after Imelda.

Gloria started after them on foot, but the other American took hold of her arm. "I think we should just let them be," he suggested. "Ryan knows what he is doing."

Gloria looked at him in the eye and then at his hand on her arm. The man quickly let go of her arm, extended his hand, and introduced himself, "Hi, I'm Rob, Ryan's cousin."

Gloria looked again into his eyes, noticed this time that they were blue, and smiled as she shook his hand.

Imelda saw Ryan chasing after her.

"Imbecile," Imelda thought to herself. "How dare he," she thought.

She kicked Kronos harder, and he went into a full gallop. Imelda, an experienced rider, safely maneuvered the jumps over fallen tree limbs and shrubs. Ryan, not to be outdone, cleared them just as easily. Ryan's actions only irritated Imelda more.

She had to lose him quickly. Acting brashly, she pushed Kronos to go faster through the tall *talahib* grass. She briefly turned over her shoulder to see if she had lost Ryan and did not notice that there was something in the grass that spooked Kronos. The horse reared and suddenly bucked.

Caught by surprise, Imelda dropped the reins and fell forward, clutching Kronos' neck. She tried desperately to get her bearings when she felt a strong arm pull her off Kronos. Imelda found herself on Ryan's horse.

And just like that, Kronos suddenly stopped moving.

After ensuring that Imelda was squarely seated on the saddle, Ryan dismounted. Still holding the reins of his horse, he slowly approached Kronos.

"There, there, Kronos," said Ryan calmly, gently picking up the reins. He proceeded to pat him on the neck. With both reins securely in his hand, Ryan led the horses out of the *talahib* grass.

As soon as they cleared the grass, Imelda jumped off to dismount. "Give me back my horse," she demanded.

"You're welcome," Ryan said, handing her the reins.

"Amazing!" exclaimed Imelda. "If you had not come after us, we would have been all right," she grumbled as she made her way back to the stables.

"If I had not come after you just in time, you would have fallen off Kronos," Ryan corrected as he joined Imelda's side.

Ryan and his wisecracks only annoyed Imelda further. Seeing no point in making a retort, she took off, but Ryan, quiet now, followed. Imelda was fuming and did not desire another moment of Ryan's company. She stopped and prepared to mount Kronos again, but the horse was not cooperating.

"Imelda," Don Fulgencio called out. "There you are. I've been looking for you two."

"Yes, Papa," answered Imelda.

"I see you have met Ryan and Kronos," Don Fulgencio said reaching over to pat Kronos.

Kronos moved his head up and down as if to say yes. The stallion then started sniffing Don Fulgencio, looking for a treat.

"A-ha! You are a smart one," exclaimed Don Fulgencio as he pulled a carrot from his pocket. "You know I have something for you."

"Imelda, this is Rob, Ryan's cousin," said Don Fulgencio as he tapped Rob's shoulder.

"Hello, Imelda," Rob said, extending his hand. Imelda shook his hand.

"Gloria, this is Ryan. Ryan, this is my niece, Gloria." Don Fulgencio said as he pointed toward Gloria.

Ryan extended his hand to Gloria, "Pleased to meet you," he said.

"Now that we have all the introductions out of the way, we should go back to the house for *merienda*," said Don Fulgencio, motioning to the main house.

"Ignacio, take Kronos back to the stables. Imelda, go on ahead and freshen up. Gloria will go with you to help. We will meet you on the veranda," instructed Don Fulgencio.

"Yes, Papa," said Imelda, grabbing Gloria's hand and started back for the main house.

Imelda and Gloria soon rejoined the men on the veranda. *Yaya* Pacing brought a tray of finger sandwiches and *calamansi* juice. Don

Fulgencio lit a cigar. Both Ryan and Rob were casually reclining on the rattan chairs while listening to Don Fulgencio when they all stood up to welcome the women.

"I am glad you joined us," Ryan said, smiling at Imelda.

Unimpressed, Imelda nodded and tugged on Gloria's hand.

Rob was trying to catch Gloria's attention with a small wave of his hand, but Imelda was still pulling at her. Gloria shot a quick frown of annoyance at her cousin.

"Yes, Imelda?" Gloria intoned.

"You asked me to remind you to inform our guests that we have plans for later today," Imelda answered.

"Oh, yes," Gloria confirmed. "We were invited to go to Estela's dinner party tonight."

"Estela is having a party tonight?" asked Don Fulgencio.

"Yes, Papa," replied Imelda.

"That's perfect!" exclaimed Don Fulgencio. "I will send word to her to have two places added at her table for Ryan and Rob."

"But Papa," Imelda objected, "I believe it is too late to make such an accommodation."

"Nonsense!" Don Fulgencio responded. "Ryan and Rob will escort you girls to Estela's dinner party."

"I hate to impose on anyone, Don Fulgencio," exclaimed Ryan.

"It's alright, Ryan. They will make room. Actually, I shall send word now."

"Pacing!" Don Fulgencio called out, ranging the tiny bell beside him.

Yaya Pacing came to the veranda quickly.

Don Fulgencio gave her instructions to have both Ryan and Rob included at the dinner party. He then turned to the women and said, "Well, I think it's time for you ladies to primp for the party."

He then turned to the men and asked, "I trust you have appropriate dinner attire for this evening. If not, Pacing can help you find something suitable."

The men stood up as Gloria and Imelda took their leave. After excusing themselves from Don Fulgencio, Rob and Ryan departed as well, following Pacing to the tailor.

As soon as they were out of earshot, Gloria whispered to Imelda, "I told you so. We are not going to be rid of them any time soon."

Imelda made a sour face and retorted, "How I wish we could rid of them sooner. That Ryan is so cocky. He thinks he knows everything. So pushy."

"Rob is alright. But, then again, all he does is follow Ryan. I think *Tio* Fule likes them," said Gloria.

That statement only irritated Imelda more as they walked to their room to prepare for the dinner party.

Yaya Pacing had already laid out their gowns on their beds. Their beaded slippers were on the floor next to their outfits. On the ironing board, the charcoal pressing iron had hot coals in it with very long machine cut iron nails.

Carefully, Gloria and Imelda each removed a hot iron nail, let it cool a moment, and then wrapped it with a small section of their hair. They gave their locks a moment to set then pulled out the nails, letting their new curls fall to their shoulders.

"*Aray!*" Imelda cried out as she dropped the hot nail.

"Imelda, are you okay? Let me see your hand," Gloria demanded.

"It's not so bad. I let go of the nail when I felt it was hotter than I thought it was," Imelda explained.

"I hope *Yaya* Pacing was able to get a lot of ice from the ice plant. I can ask her to bring ice for your burn," Gloria said as she rang her bell.

When *Yaya* Pacing came, Gloria explained what had happened. She rushed out and quickly returned with a *tabo* of ice filled with water. Imelda soaked her blistering finger in the *tabo*.

Yaya Pacing stayed to help them finish curling their hair. Afterward, Imelda gently combed her hair away from her face and fastened it with a *peineta* made of tortoiseshell. Gloria did the same with her hair, but with a wooden comb inlaid with mother of pearl.

"I remember this comb belonged to your mother, Doña Marietta," *Yaya* Pacing said as she admired the comb on Imelda's hair.

The two women powdered their faces and sprayed perfume on their necks and wrists before stepping into their gowns and slippers. They picked up the handkerchiefs and fans that waited atop their dresser.

Both Gloria and Imelda looked into the mirror, turning around to make sure they looked beautiful for the party. It was a process, but it was well worth the effort.

Ryan was changing into the *barong tagalog* that *Yaya* Pacing had brought in when he blurted, "I like her! She is so beautiful and spirited."

Rob turned to look at him and asked, "You are not talking about a horse, are you?"

"Of course not!" exclaimed Ryan. "Imelda, I am talking about her." He was obviously thinking of her and she had left him awestruck.

"Oh, boy. Imelda is not like one of your horses. You cannot simply tame that one. Did you see her? Clearly, she is an athlete and very headstrong. She will not come willingly," Rob said as he combed his hair.

"I know. I can see it in Imelda's eyes. There is fire in it! She knows what she wants, and she has that fight in her," Ryan said.

"We are talking about Imelda, right? Gloria seems amiable. She may be easier to attain." Rob suggested as he put on his *barong tagalog*.

"Ah, but she is no Imelda. I am setting my eyes on her," Ryan said as he finished buttoning up his *barong*.

"Good luck. It's not going to be easy. I can see that now," Rob chuckled.

Ryan looked into the mirror and said, "She will come around. You will see."

HOW DARE YOU

"Imelda, I know you are guarding this secret very fiercely. But at what cost? I'm dying. We should not stay silent because it only victimizes us again over and over. We were the oppressed here," Gloria pleaded from her hospital bed.

Imelda was reading a magazine by Gloria's bedside. She put the magazine down and quickly looked around to make sure there was no one within earshot.

"Shush, Gloria. Someone might hear you," cautioned Imelda. "You are on edge. Should I get you more morphine?"

Imelda stood up and started to look for the nurse call button. She found it tucked in slightly underneath Gloria. As Imelda was about to pull it out and push the call button, Gloria placed her hand on top of Imelda's.

"You are strong, Imelda. You can and will come out of this better than before. Ryan is standing by your side. He is there for you whether you want him to be or not. I do not think this revelation will make him leave you if that is your concern," Gloria pressed on.

"Gloria, please stop! I'm doing my best to handle this. Encouraging my daughter is not helping, but if you and Adele want to change the world, go ahead and do it, but please do not include me. I've made my peace," Imelda insisted, walking away towards the window.

San Francisco was beginning to wake up. Imelda looked out the window and closed her eyes, letting the sun's warm rays envelop her.

"Lord, please give me the strength," she whispered to herself.

Imelda opened her eyes and gazed out the window again. A boy was riding a bicycle up the hill, flinging a rolled newspaper at each building. She watched a small group of children cheerfully chatting as they held on to their book bags while they walked to school. A man was running downhill to catch his bus a block away. A couple of senior women were pushing their carts headed to the grocery. Yes, Imelda would rather have been down there instead of being in the room with Gloria right now.

"Really? You are stuck with Ryan even when you are not crazy about him. Let's face it, he gets on your nerves. You are too afraid to move out of your security blanket. You have put yourself in a box. No past, no future. You created your own space. So now you are stuck. The box is stifling you. You can't breathe and can't escape. You are trapped," Gloria said, her tone slightly stronger now.

"Really?" Imelda reacted, getting annoyed. "How do you know the state of my marriage? I am perfectly fine. Ryan is not the best, but we get along. We respect each other enough to not pry into each other's affairs."

But that did not keep Gloria from badgering her.

"And you call that a happy marriage? Where is the passion? The living life with gusto. Staying at home day in, day out doing menial things is not living! It's like doing time before death!"

"Really, at our age?" Imelda responded emphatically. "We had our fun. We are now settling down."

"Bullshit!" Gloria kept going. "The Imelda I knew had fire in her belly! She was adventurous, and she was *mataray*! No one can tell her what to do. She decided what she wanted and went for it if she chose, but you lost your teeth!"

Imelda started to walk away from Gloria.

"I don't know what you are talking about, Gloria."

"Uh, please, Imelda. The Imelda I knew was *suplada*! *Tio* Fule made sure she was smart and confident. It enabled her to be self-assured and very competent. You may have been a bit introverted, but it was definitely not because you were shy but quite the opposite."

"What are you babbling about?" asked Imelda.

"You have changed so much. I can see that Ryan irritates you with his canned responses. He bores you to death. I know there is still so much life in you, and yet you choose to be with him, a security blanket. You do not need him. You are very independent! It's like he's chained you and will drag you down into the life of oblivion and nothingness."

"Just stop, ok," Imelda pleaded. "I've made my choice, and I am good with it."

Gloria started to cough. Imelda poured a glass of water and put a straw in it. She handed it to Gloria and watched her take a sip. Gloria closed her eyes and contemplated on what to say next.

When Gloria opened her eyes, she was calm.

"Seriously, Imelda, don't settle. Life is much too short. You still have so much to live for. Leave Ryan and make something for yourself. You can, you know. It's just a matter of walking out the door and closing it behind you."

Imelda was sitting down looking for a handkerchief in her purse.

"Gloria, I love you, but you do not know what you are talking about."

The cousins sat in silence for a few minutes, and the room felt heavy with purpose. Like battling chess players weighing their options and planning their next move, Gloria and Imelda were each quietly thinking of what to say next.

"Imelda, we're old now, but it doesn't mean we are dead," Gloria said. "Whether Ryan leaves you or supports you because of what happened to us during our captivity doesn't matter. You deserve to have your voice. I need you to rise up and do more than just be heard. I want you to take hold of the situation and control the narrative. Take it a step further. Do not let your fear dictate your actions. Let your voice be the instrument of change…"

Gloria paused to collect her thoughts. In her heart, she knew the importance of Imelda's coming out. She carefully considered how to impart the gravity of the situation and elicit the response required to evoke change.

"We are the casualty of war," she continued. "You and I must go beyond being victims and be the survivors that take control of our reality and be the bridge for all the comfort women. To start, we should come together and demand an apology. We need to do this, especially for all of us women. We need to stick together and stand up in unity against the injustice done to us. We, the women, must take an active hand on this. We must be able to say no and be respected for that choice. Rape is violent, and no woman should ever go through it."

Imelda was still not persuaded.

"And what? Washing my dirty linen in public will change that? I do not need their pity," she said.

"We are not asking for pity. We want respect! There rests the difference and it will begin once the Japanese acknowledge what they have done. Every one of us had a bright future ahead before they showed up. They took our future away. It is an atrocity of war," Gloria replied.

"Exactly! It is an atrocity that should be buried. Gloria, why bring up something so ugly and dirty?"

"Imelda, we need to be cleansed! We do not need to live in shame. We did not ask for it."

Imelda swung around to face Gloria and reminded her, "I'm sorry, but you have been very vocal about this from day one and look where it has led you."

"Ah, yes. I am the branded one, the spoiled goods that no one wanted and, yet I managed to have three husbands. I lived, loved, and then some," Gloria replied as she was reaching her water.

Imelda walked over to help her. She took the plastic cup after Gloria took a sip and gently put it on the table.

Imelda caught a breath before continuing, "Gloria, maybe you are high or something. Stop talking! You are just raking over old wounds."

Gloria adjusted her bed by pushing the button next to her bed so she could sit up.

"You know, Imelda, my ex-husbands couldn't handle me! They couldn't handle me," she exclaimed. "I was more a woman than they could ever be men. How stupid can they be to try to find a woman just like their mommies who would indulge them? Well, I called them out on their shit to their faces, and they acted like little boys who surely could not handle the truth. Especially that idiot second husband of mine! They will never grow up!"

"Okay, that's it! I think you're delirious or extremely high."

Imelda turned and started to leave the room to get help for Gloria.

"Imelda, mark my words. Years from now, women will have to decide for themselves what it is that they want and go for it, but we can start that conversation now. We should stand up and be counted."

"Counted for what? Do you honestly think they will take us seriously? They will sit and pretend to listen, and then what? Go back to their little boy's club, smoke a few cigars, and call it a day," Imelda exclaimed as she walked back to Gloria's bedside.

Gloria looked squarely at Imelda.

"Yes, but at least we put them on notice."

They both paused and continued to look at one another. Neither wanted to argue with the other. Not over this.

"Imelda," Gloria started to say. "We need to do something. Future generations will look at this moment and say this was the pivotal moment for all women. We woke up and stood up against those pigs! We called upon our shared experiences and banded together to push the envelope."

"So, this is now a crusade?" retorted Imelda as she threw her hands up in the air.

"Call it what you want, but it should stop here with us. We should be able to say stop and no more. Women are more than just mothers, *yayas*, and sex slaves. We need to be treated as equals and not as objects. We are human, and history cannot and should not be allowed to repeat itself. By staying quiet, we are saying yes; we were brutalized this way, and it is okay. Well, it is not okay. No one's wife, mother, daughter, or sister should be subjected to sexual abuse, and yes, rape is one of them," exclaimed Gloria adamantly.

Imelda leaned closer on Gloria's bed.

"Gloria, I was there, and I know, but why push and expose this? Is it worth the ridicule? The abandonment by friends and family who do not want to be part of this? Who would listen to a handful of Filipinas and be moved to do something about this?"

"That's the problem. Why stay in the shadows? Yes, we may never get what we want. I may never get to see or hear the apology, but let it be known that I asked for it. I asked for myself and all of my Filipina sisters. We might not get it, but we did demand it! We cannot let future generations go through what we suffered," Gloria said emphatically.

"Gloria, a handful of women will not be enough. You will need more women and more supporters," Imelda explained as she reached over to hold Gloria's hand.

"But that is a start," Gloria uttered with conviction. She closed her eyes to think of a way to best illustrate this to her cousin.

"Remember what *Tio* Fule said about the *walis tingting*?" Gloria reminded Imelda. "He said that it is easy to break one *tingting* but tied together as a bunch, the *walis tingting* cannot be broken in half. I may be one of many victims, but if we can band together and stand up for ourselves, then we have a chance to change the future. If not for ourselves, we need to do it for future generations of women."

Imelda held her cousin's frail shoulder as she closed her eyes briefly to remember Don Fulgencio's face. He did say that. For him, strength was in numbers, but this was one battle she did not want to be a part of at all. She stood up and walked toward the door as if by merely walking away from Gloria, it would end this distasteful discussion.

"You have to do something, Imelda. You can no longer sit on the fence on this matter. You have to join the fight against those Japanese pigs. They cannot treat us, the Filipinas, like they treat their women. We are not mere objects; we are living, breathing human beings who have a right to be treated as equals. Demand an apology! Make them tell the truth. They raped us, and they have hell to pay, and it starts with an apology!" Gloria expressed forcefully.

Imelda was holding the doorknob when she paused, turned around and faced Gloria. "I'm going to get help, but please stop talking about the Japanese."

"Those Japanese pigs!" Gloria scoffed as she started to cough repeatedly.

Imelda ran back to hand the glass of water to Gloria.

"Now look at who is being bitter," Imelda pointed out.

Gloria took a sip, caught her breath, and took a longer sip before handing the glass back to Imelda. "I am not bitter. I am just calling out their shit. They did this to me, they have to pay, and I am not talking about money. I want my dignity back! I want to be made whole again."

"And a public apology will make all of that go away? Do you

think a few spoken words will wipe away the years of shame? Can they bring back the loved ones who left because of the shame they felt?" Imelda asked her cousin.

"Again, Imelda, those who supposedly left me because of the shame they felt are total idiots! I do not need them if they cannot stand up for me. If they treat me like a blight, if they cannot support me, I have no need for them," Gloria answered firmly.

Gloria could not help remembering what happened many years ago when she was still married to her first husband, Diego. It was the day she and her boys, Kent and Bruce, came home from the department store. Bruce was four years old, and Kent was two and a half years old…

When she opened the door to her house, they were startled to see pieces of luggage on the foyer. Even the boys' toys were there. Diego was there with his hands on his waist. Gloria went up to kiss him, but Diego held his hand up to stop her.

"Is it true?" Diego asked Gloria with consternation

Gloria looked at him with bewilderment. "What do you mean?".

"Did you tell the women at the boys' school that you were a comfort woman?" Diego asked her angrily.

"Yes, I did," Gloria replied.

No sooner did she answer that Diego slapped her! Their two boys ran to Gloria's side and began to cry.

"What the hell were you thinking, telling people that you were a comfort woman?!" Diego continued shouting.

Gloria's cheek was bright red and tears were rolling down her face. You can see the mark Diego's hand left on her face.

"But it is the truth," she answered between sobs.

"I told you never to tell anyone!" Diego retorted. "Now they know! You are an embarrassment, and, now, you make the boys and me an embarrassment!"

Diego was pacing the room wildly like a caged animal ready to pounce; he was very agitated as he took a swig of his whiskey straight from the bottle. For him, there was no need to be proper anymore since everything turned into garbage. His reputation is now completely and utterly damaged!

"*Wala kang hiya!*" he shouted while pointing a derisive finger at Gloria. "Have you no shame?"

Diego picked up a suitcase and threw it out the door. "Take your things and never come back!" he shouted angrily.

"Diego, please stop," Gloria begged him as she tried to stop him.

"I told you to never tell anyone! Do you know how humiliating it is for me? My wife was a sex slave! Just how many men have you had? You are so dirty! I should not even touch you!" Diego was screaming furiously.

"It is not like I had a choice!" Gloria answered back with anger slowly creeping in her voice. "You were not the one assaulted many times over! I was! And, talk about pain, it was not you who was hit, punched, and thrown about like a rag doll — demeaned in every possible way. It was I!" she said defiantly.

With the anger and rage she has suppressed for many years coming to a head, it suddenly dawned on Gloria that there was nothing to be ashamed anymore; the abuses she suffered was not her fault and she should not be paying for it.

Gloria immediately held on to her boys.

"Kent and Bruce are coming with me!"

The boys were sobbing loudly. Kent was holding on to Gloria's legs while Bruce stood there, unsure of what to do. He looked so lost and afraid.

"Take them! I do not want them," Diego exclaimed. His eyes fiery like they were raging. The stench of alcohol was on his breath. "They are tainted, just like you!"

This time Bruce ran up to his dad to hold on to him but Diego forcibly pushed him away. "No, go away. I do not even know if you are mine!" Diego sneered at Bruce.

Gloria was still holding on to Kent when Diego shoved her aside to continue throwing their belongings out the door. When he was done, Diego forcibly dragged Gloria and the boys out of their home. Then he swung the door shut and locked it.

"Daddy!" cried Bruce as he rapped on the door with his little hands. "Please, Daddy. I will be good. Please let me back in," he begged desperately.

Gloria reached out to him, but Bruce flinches at her touch. "This is all your fault," he yelled at his mom.

Bruce continued to rap on the door begging Diego to open it and let him in. But the door remained shut.

There was nothing Gloria could do to console Bruce. They were both heartbroken. Even the toddler, Kent, was crying continuously on her shoulder, mercifully unaware of what was happening.

Later that evening, Imelda opened her door to see Gloria and the boys. She swiftly embraced Gloria while she cried on her shoulder. Neither said anything. They held each other for as long they needed.

Imelda asked Ryan to pay the taxi and help bring their things to the cottage behind the main house.

"Bruce, this will be your new home," she showed the cottage to Bruce with a smile.

Bruce looked at her and said defiantly, "This is not my home! I want to go back to my dad!"

"Hey, buddy," Ryan exclaimed as he ran toward Bruce and put his hand on his shoulder. "I understand. Things are a little crazy now. Why don't we just take a break and we can work something out later. In the meantime, Auntie Imelda baked some cookies. I think they are ready to eat. Let's get some. Sounds good?"

Bruce looked at Ryan intently as if to judge how sincere he was. He reluctantly nodded as he entered the cottage to get cookies with Ryan.

Gloria was carrying Kent when she walked into the cottage. She gently put the sleeping Kent on the sofa and covered him with a throw blanket. Gloria kissed him on the forehead. Kent moved his head slightly.

She sat down next to him and then covered her face with her hands and cried quietly. It was over with her and Diego. Her marriage was over through no fault of her own. She was now alone with two little boys to raise by herself.

Gloria's eyes brimmed with tears as she recollected that painful moment in her life. She was more concerned for her boys.

It was Imelda's voice that pulled her from her reverie.

"And that is why you are all alone. Some things you have keep to yourself. You and your need to overshare," Imelda admonished her, unaware that Gloria's mind was somewhere else.

That remark only drew rebuke from Gloria.

"And be like you, Imelda? All stiff and proper," Gloria retorted. "Have they, our so-called friends and family, looked underneath that perfect veil of yours? You are cracking up Imelda. Slowly but surely you are, and when the dam breaks, what will you do?"

"I don't know, but it will not happen today or tomorrow. Let's worry about you. I told Adele to stop goading you on and on about those Japanese. The past is the past. Let it rest," Imelda said, keeping her hand on Gloria's shoulder.

Gloria took Imelda's hand with her own and looked into cousin's eyes, saying solemnly, "But I will not rest in peace, and neither should you. This was not our fault, but theirs, and they should pay. The atrocities they committed against us cannot be repeated in the future. That evil needs to leave this world when we do, never to be seen again..."

Beep. Beep.

A beeping sound interrupted Gloria. One of her monitoring devices went off. She lost consciousness.

The machines' alarms were sounding off.

Imelda started to scream. "Nurse! Nurse! Help! She passed out," Imelda cried out.

Nurses rushed in. "Call the doctor stat!" exclaimed one nurse to another.

The same nurse turned to Imelda and said, "Mrs. Makena, you should leave the room. Let us do our best for her."

Imelda hurriedly made her way to the door but stayed just outside Gloria's room.

"Just like what happened to Papa," Imelda said to herself while starting to remember the girl she once was...

Imelda was still scolding Gloria for running out of the basement as they climbed off the tree.

"We have to hurry!" said Imelda. "It is not safe. We should get back to the basement before we run into another group of Japanese soldiers."

Gloria walked quickly behind Imelda, making sure to look around for soldiers.

Soon they were just outside the back of their home. They moved the pieces of wood and broken furniture that covered the door. Then, they swiftly opened the door. After they went through the door, they pulled the same broken furniture over to cover it up again before closing the door.

Yaya Pacing, who looked overly distressed, promptly ran up to Imelda and Gloria.

"I'm so glad you are back. Something happened to Don Fulgencio. I think it's really bad," she said tearfully.

The girls ran to the other end of the basement to see Dr. Jose whispering to Don Fulgencio.

Dr. Jose walked towards them and told them that Don Fulgencio did not have much time left.

Imelda ran to Don Fulgencio quickly. He was propped up by

pillows as he lay on the *papag*. His eyes were half-open. Drool was pooling on one side of his mouth. One can clearly hear his breathing sounded irregular and labored.

"Papa, do not leave me," cried Imelda clinging to her papa's hand. "I need you. I wouldn't know what to do."

"*Hija*, don't worry. I will always be with you, whatever happens." Don Fulgencio said softly.

"But Papa, I promise not to leave you again. I do not want to be without you," cried Imelda kneeling next to him, tears falling uncontrollably.

"*Tio* Fule, I'm so sorry I ran out." Gloria cried as she held on to his hand.

"Shush," Don Fulgencio said to Gloria. "It's okay. I understand. These are very trying times."

Don Fulgencio took the hands of both girls and put them together. He covered them with his own and said, "I want you girls to stay together, especially now. Lean on each other and protect each other. You are closer than actual sisters," he struggled to look at both girls.

"Gloria," said Don Fulgencio, "I promised your mom, my dearest sister before she passed that I would take care of you. I'm so sorry I cannot keep that promise." A tear fell from Don Fulgencio's eye.

"No, *Tio* Fule, you did more than take care of me. Mama is happy. No one else could have done better." Gloria reassured him as she held on tightly to his hand.

"Promise me that you will look after each other," Don Fulgencio requested with all sincerity.

Both girls nodded solemnly, and all three held hands tightly.

There was a brief silence. Each was saying a prayer in their hearts. No one dared to say anything out loud for fear that the moment would be lost. Then it happened. Don Fulgencio's hand went limp and fell off the girls' hands.

"Papa!" Imelda wailed as tears poured down her eyes like a deluge.

The girls continued to hold hands as they cried over Don Fulgencio.

MY FIRST TIME

Kronos was navigating the brook when the horse stopped and would not go any further. Imelda kept pushing him to go but to no avail. Kronos resisted every attempt.

"What's wrong, Kronos?" asked Imelda as she gently stroked Kronos' neck.

She was about to dismount when another rider approached.

"Good morning," the rider said.

"Good morning," replied Imelda as she desperately tried to make Kronos move.

"Need help?" he asked as he got closer to Imelda.

"I was trying to cross but Kronos does not want to move," Imelda answered.

The rider swiftly dismounted and tied his own horse to his belt. He then carefully approached Kronos.

"There must be something in the water that he does not like," he said as he waded in the water to get closer to Kronos.

"Hey, Kronos. It's ok. Come on now. I will walk you through," he said as he talked to Kronos. No sooner after he said that, he missed a step and fell down into the water.

Imelda quickly dismounted to help him, but she too fell into the deep water.

He instantly reemerged as his horse pulled him out. Seeing that Imelda was missing, he dove back into the water to find her. They both came out of the water together and he guided her back to where their horses stood waiting.

They took one look at each other and started to laugh.

"You know it is not advisable to be riding alone," he said as he helped her onto a big rock.

"I know," Imelda answered. "Papa told me many times."

"And yet here you are," he said as he smiled.

Imelda blushed and looked down.

"My name is Kenji," he said while extending his hand.

"Imelda," she answered as she shook his hand.

"Ah, the famous Imelda. Don Fulgencio's daughter!" Kenji exclaimed.

"You know my Papa?" she asked.

"Yes, I do. As a matter of fact, I have an appointment to see your father later this afternoon." Kenji said as he noticed Imelda shiver.

Kenji walked to his horse and reached for his pack. He then pulled out a towel and a shirt.

"Here, take these," Kenji said as he handed the items to Imelda. "You can change behind that tree. I won't look. You have to get out of that wet shirt, or you will catch a cold."

Imelda gladly took the shirt and towel and walked behind the tree as Kenji turned to face the other way.

"I thought I would be the only rider out this early," Kenji exclaimed.

"I like to get out at dawn. The air is crisp, and there is no one to bother me," she answered as she changed.

"Well, sorry to bother you then," Kenji replied. "I know what it is like to be alone with your thoughts and ride free in peace."

"Oh no, you saved me!" said Imelda emerging from behind the tree. "I am grateful."

She was watching her steps very closely as she traced her way back to where Kenji was standing that by the time she looked up she almost bumped into him. They briefly smiled at each other, and each took a step back.

"I have to be getting back," Imelda said. "They will be looking for me."

"Go ahead. Be careful on your way back." Kenji replied with a smile on his face.

Imelda gave Kenji his towel. She put her foot on the stirrup, while Kenji held on to Kronos. With one swing, Imelda was on Kronos.

"Thank you again," she said. "I will have your shirt sent to you."

"No worries. Keep it, throw it away, whatever." Kenji said. "I hope to see you again."

"Perhaps," Imelda answered coyly as she rode away.

"There you are!" exclaimed *Yaya* Pacing when Imelda walked inside.

"Is that Imelda, *Yaya*?" called out Gloria as she walked towards *Yaya* Pacing.

Imelda entered the room sheepishly with a smile on her face.

"What are you wearing?" asked Gloria as she gave Imelda a look over. "Is that a man's shirt?!" exclaimed Gloria.

"Shush," said Imelda as she started to undress. "I have to take a bath," she said as she pulled off her water-logged boots.

"*Santa Maria*! What happened to you?" exclaimed *Yaya* Pacing.

"*Yaya*. I am ok." Imelda reassured her.

"Oh, you're in trouble now," Gloria taunted. "Just wait till *Tio* Fule finds out."

Imelda abruptly turned to Gloria. "Papa will not hear of this, understand!" she exclaimed as she stared at Gloria sternly.

Imelda was still musing over the morning's event as she walked into the veranda to see her Papa smoking a cigar. Catching sight of her, Don Fulgencio stood up. As she approached him, she realized he wasn't alone.

"Ah, *Hija*. There you are!" he said as he reached to her to receive a kiss on both cheeks.

He stepped to his right and introduced Imelda to his companion. "Imelda, this is Kenji. He was part of the Japanese Olympic equestrian delegation."

Kenji extended his hand to Imelda. "So nice to make your acquaintance," he said smiling.

Imelda was surprised but shook his hand anyway, not saying anything. She proceeded to take a seat next to her Papa. Both men then proceeded to take their seats.

"Imelda, honey. I am so happy that Kenji is here. I told him that you love riding horses so much. He may be able to give you some pointers to improve your riding skills." Don Fulgencio boasted.

"Don Fulgencio, I am sure your daughter is quite an accomplished rider. No need for input from me." Kenji assured him.

Perfecto stood within view of Don Fulgencio. "Come here, Perfecto," motioned Don Fulgencio.

"Don Fulgencio, the American Ryan is here to see the *Señorita*," announced Perfecto.

"Well, bring him in," said Don Fulgencio.

Perfecto led Ryan into the veranda. He had a bouquet of exotic-looking flowers in his hand.

"Good afternoon Don Fulgencio and Imelda," said Ryan. "I brought these for you, Imelda. These orchids grow profusely in my home in Hawaii," he said as he gave her the flowers.

"These are beautiful. Thank you," said Imelda admiring the

flowers.

"Ryan, this is Kenji. Kenji, this is Ryan," Don Fulgencio said as he introduced them to each other. Both men shook hands, acknowledging one another.

"Well, Imelda, why don't you show Ryan our local orchids," instructed Don Fulgencio. "Kenji and I have other business to discuss."

Imelda stood up, and the men stood up too to let Imelda pass through. She was looking down at the flowers when she said goodbye to Kenji, "It was nice meeting you."

"The pleasure is mine," replied Kenji.

Imelda smiled and started to walk to the garden with Ryan.

"You're here!" called out Kenji.

"You are too," answered Imelda as she turned her horse around to face Kenji.

"I was hoping I'd catch you here," replied Kenji as he rode closer to her.

"Why?" asked Imelda.

"Come on. You know why," Kenji said with a smile then continued, "So you have a riding partner. Someone has to keep an eye on you in case ..."

"Haha! If I remember correctly, you needed help first," taunted Imelda.

"Ah, you forget! That was only because you needed help crossing the river," corrected Kenji as he turned his horse to face Imelda directly.

She paused to think of how to answer him.

"Details, details," exclaimed Kenji as he made his horse turn to his side to face forward.

"So, let's go," said Kenji.

"Go where?" asked Imelda.

"Riding, silly," Kenji cracked as he kicked his horse and rode away.

And off they went.

The morning rides together turned into an almost daily occurrence. Sometimes, Kenji and Imelda would get off their horses to give them a drink or a treat. They would sit on a rock or under a tree and talk. Occasionally, laughter would break up their quiet talks. Imelda and Kenji would sometimes discuss serious matters. Kenji could be seen staring at Imelda, quietly impressed with her fervor and conviction. Imelda, on the other hand, was drawn to his charisma and energy. Their early morning rides continued for months.

"I have to see you tonight. I have something very special to tell you," Kenji told Imelda.

"Oh. Tell me now then," replied Imelda riding alongside him.

"No. Like I said, it's special," insisted Kenji.

"Where? I need to be properly chaperoned."

"Can it be just us?" Kenji asked earnestly.

"I do not know how," she replied as she looked down.

"I rented a place a bit off the beaten track, so to speak. Do you know the old Lucio farm? I rented the cottage on the southwest corner. Meet me there tonight," he said.

Imelda hesitated, "I don't know. I don't think I can get away."

Kenji stopped his horse and looked squarely at Imelda. "Please. It's important. I'll see you tonight," he said. And with that, Kenji rode away before Imelda could say anything.

Imelda reached the top of the staircase and saw Gloria embroidering by the window, silently humming as she worked. A gentle breeze caused the curtains to billow out and back softly.

"Gloria, I need your help!" exclaimed Imelda.

"Help with what?" asked Gloria, looking up from her work. "You finally want to learn embroidery?"

"No, not that," answered Imelda sitting down next to Gloria. "I need to get away tonight. When *Yaya* Pacing comes, tell her I am in bed with a cold or something."

"I don't like this. What if something happens to you?" asked Gloria putting down her embroidery hoop.

Imelda reached for Gloria's hand and said, "Nothing will happen. I will be alright. Promise."

Gloria thought about it. *"How much trouble can she get into anyway?"* She asked herself.

"What is taking her so long to think about it," Imelda said to herself.

After what seemed like an eternity to Imelda, Gloria finally said, "Ok. *Ingat*"

Imelda reached the Lucio property quickly. She scanned the area for the cottage that Kenji mentioned. There it was in the southwest corner as he had said it would be. There was a light coming out of the window. As she got closer, she could smell something nice coming from the cottage.

On the side of the cottage, Imelda saw Kenji's horse tied to a post. Imelda tied Kronos next to his horse. She tidied her blouse before she walked to the door. Imelda paused for a minute before she raised her hand to knock. As she was about to turn her back to walk away, Kenji opened the door.

"You're here!" he exclaimed happily.

Imelda smiled briefly, walking tentatively inside. "You are, too!" she answered.

"What smells so good?" Imelda asked.

"Oh, you noticed. I cooked dinner for us. Nothing grand. Pretty simple, in fact," Kenji explained.

He took Imelda's hand and led her to the table. "Here, have a seat," he said, pulling out a seat for her.

"You did all of this?" Imelda gasped.

"Yes. Come on, let's eat. I don't know if you have ever tried sake, but I brought some back from Japan," Kenji asked, showing her the bottle.

As Imelda sat down, she marveled at the table. In the middle of the table was a lantern. Smaller candles were around it. Flowers lay scattered on the table. Instead of forks, there were sticks.

"These are chopsticks. It's easy when you get the hang of it. Here let me show you," Kenji said as he leaned close to Imelda. He was so close that he could smell her perfume.

He took her hand and placed the chopsticks between her fingers. "I know it looks complicated but bear with me," explained Kenji. "You hold both sticks between your thumb and pointer finger, then put your middle finger in between both sticks. Here you go."

It didn't take Imelda long to get the chopsticks to work for her.

"See," said Kenji. "You're a natural!"

"It's like crocheting but with an extra needle," answered Imelda.

"Then let's drink to this," Kenji said, pouring sake into two tiny cups. He handed a cup to Imelda and then raised his own, exclaiming, "*Kanpai!*"

"*Kanpai,*" cheered Imelda.

Imelda looked at Kenji's face. "*He seems incredibly happy,*" she thought to herself. "*Oh no. I think he is going to propose! This cannot happen! We are perfect the way we are. If he says something, it will ruin everything. It will cause me to acknowledge my feelings and I am not ready yet. I will have to respond, and the casual flirting and spending time together will change. I want the dynamics of how we spend time together the way it is. To define it now will change everything. I am not ready!*"

"Now, for that special matter that I want to talk to you about," Kenji started to say.

"Let's enjoy this meal first. It's incredibly tasty," interrupted Imelda as she poured more sake into their individual cups. "*Kanpai*"

And that was how the rest of the evening went. Every time Kenji would start to bring up what he wanted to say, Imelda would divert him and take a shot of sake.

Soon after, they finished their meal and consumed more than three bottles of sake. Imelda was making her way to leave when Kenji called out, "Where are you going?"

"I'm going home," she answered.

"Wait," he said as he tried to stand up, "Let me take you home." Kenji was definitely inebriated. He needed to hold on to the chair just to be able to stand.

"I'm afraid you are too drunk to do that," Imelda affirmed with a giggle.

"Well, I think you are right," he said as he sat down again. "We both had a lot to drink. I should escort you home. Let's take a short nap. Can't be falling off our horses now."

"I guess. I am a bit tipsy, too," Imelda admitted as she sat down on the sofa.

"Ok, let's do this," said Kenji. "I will take a nap here, and you take a nap there. I promise I won't do anything foolish."

Imelda sighed and nodded okay.

The weight of Kenji on top of her woke Imelda up. He had managed to take off her underwear, and now he was taking advantage of her. She could not move because he held her down as he proceeded to have intercourse with her. When he was done, he rolled off her and fell asleep. Imelda immediately pulled whatever garment she had on and turned to her side as tears rolled fiercely down her face.

Kenji began to snore when Imelda carefully got up. She picked up Kenji's clothes and boots and threw them out the window. The horses neighed as Kenji's clothing came hurtling past them. The sound caused Kenji to wake up.

"What are you doing?" Kenji asked as he realized his clothing was missing. He ran to the window where Imelda stood and looked out to find his belongings on the ground outside. He hurriedly ran out to gather them.

Imelda immediately dashed through the door and quickly mounted Kronos. She took off in the direction away from her home. She knew Kenji would try to catch up with her if she was riding towards her home, and she did not want to see him, so Imelda rode away from her home. Imelda was trying to avoid Kenji at all cost. Not after what he did!

It was almost daybreak when she reached home.

"Imelda, is that you?" whispered Gloria as she tried to open her eyes.

Imelda steeled herself as she stopped to wipe away her tears. "Yes, it's me," she said.

"What time is it? You were gone so long," said Gloria, sleepily slowly getting up from her bed.

"Shush…" Imelda said as she continued, "Go back to sleep. Let's talk in the morning."

But sleep did not come to Imelda. She was in turmoil, and sleep was the last thing on her mind. Soon enough, Imelda gave up and decided to get dressed so she could go to the veranda.

Imelda sat on one of the balcony chairs on the veranda staring beyond the trees. The morning sunrays were pouring their blessings onto the balcony. A ray of sunlight gently warmed Imelda's face, but it was all lost on her. So deep in thought was she as her eyes welled up with tears. She was contemplating the events of the night before. Was it her fault? Did she bring this upon herself? She trusted Kenji. How could he do this to her? What should she do now?

Her plan to keep Kenji from asking her to marry him backfired big time! Imelda didn't want Kenji to say anything, so she diverted his attention by toasting with drink after drink after drink. She suspected he would say something that would change the dynamic of their friendship, and she just wanted his company — someone to spend time with, uncomplicated, real, and pleasant. To talk about love in any form would have changed things. She would have to say yes or no, and then things would never have been the same, but now it is all over anyhow, just like that. And Imelda never got to hear what he was going to say to her.

"Imelda, *hija*," Don Fulgencio called out as he made his way towards her.

"Now, this is unusual," he remarked. "You are usually out riding at this time," he said as he looked at this watch. Imelda took the opportunity to wipe her tears away.

She took a step forward to kiss her papa on the cheek as Don Fulgencio leaned close.

"What's the matter, *hija*?" he asked as he pulled her chin towards him.

Imelda slowly looked up at him and desperately did her best to hold back her tears.

"You've been crying," Don Fulgencio exclaimed as he looked into her eyes. "Tell your Papa what's ailing you. Maybe it's something I can fix," he said, gently taking her hand.

Imelda would not say anything. Instead, she lurched forward to hug her papa tightly.

"Now, *hija*. You are making me worried! Did someone hurt you?" he asked as he tried to pull away so he could take a closer look at her.

Imelda tightened her embrace. Don Fulgencio quietly hugged her back and gently patted her back.

"Whatever it is, we will get through it together," Don Fulgencio reassured her. "I'm here for you when you are ready to talk."

"Thank you, Papa," Imelda whispered into his ear, hugging her papa tighter.

"*Señorita* Imelda," Ignacio called out from outside her bedroom window.

Imelda went to the window and saw both Ignacio and Kronos standing just below.

"What can I help you with?" asked Imelda.

"Don Fulgencio asked me to bring Kronos to you. He said you haven't been riding in three days. He also said that maybe if you stayed on your regular routine, you might feel better. Kronos is ready for you, *Señorita*. I think he misses you," Ignacio explained. Kronos started to neigh as if in agreement.

Imelda did not want to go, but she knew if her papa found out she didn't ride, he would ask her himself to go, and he would probably start asking more questions. "Alright, Ignacio," Imelda said in resignation. "Please wait for me."

"You're here," exclaimed Kenji as he caught a glimpse of her.

Kenji surprised Imelda, and she kicked Kronos to ride away from him.

"Wait!" Kenji shouted as he chased after Imelda.

He soon was able to catch up and managed to get ahold of Imelda's reins. "Please stop. Give me a minute to explain," he begged.

Imelda promptly dismounted and tried to run away. Kenji got off his horse and ran towards Imelda. Soon he was able to get ahold of her wrist and held her back.

"Please," Kenji said as Imelda furiously looked at him; her gaze moving to her wrist that Kenji was still holding tight.

Kenji got down on his knees and started to cry, "I'm sorry, so, so sorry. You did not deserve what I did to you. I came after you. I spent the whole morning looking for you, but you were nowhere to be found. I never meant for that to happen. I never meant to hurt you. Please forgive me." Kenji pleaded, holding on to her legs.

"I will make it up to you even if it takes a lifetime. I promise to take care of you. Can you please forgive me?" Kenji continued to beg with tears on his face.

His actions and words surprised her. Imelda was so taken aback that she herself was in tears. She did not expect this at all. Never had anything like this happened to her. She thought he would be too big to do such a thing as to beg on his knees, crying for forgiveness. A man of his stature surely does not get on his knees to beg for forgiveness. It is unheard of!

"Maybe he is not a monster after all," Imelda thought.

Kenji kept gently sobbing. His face was pressed against her legs as she stood before him. Imelda felt his warm tears as its wetness seeped into her skirt.

Imelda gently reached out to him with her right hand. Gingerly, she touched his left ear then his check. Kenji slowly looked up to her with his eyes still full of tears. Carefully, she pulled him up. Once standing, they locked in an embrace while their tears flowed freely. Neither one said anything for what seemed like a long time. They just stood there in each other's arms silently.

MY WEDDING DAY

Yaya Pacing was fixing Imelda's veil when she started crying.

"*Yaya* Pacing, why are you crying," asked Imelda.

"If only your Mama Marietta were here," *Yaya* Pacing began to say, but couldn't finish as she started to sob.

"*Yaya* Pacing," said Gloria as she placed her hand on her; she, too, almost teary-eyed now. "It is alright. I am sure *Tia* Mayet would have been so happy to see Imelda today."

"Oh, you two are terrible!" exclaimed Imelda as she pulled her handkerchief. "Now, I am going to cry too."

"Ladies, there will be absolutely no crying today!" exclaimed Don Fulgencio as he entered the room. "Now, let me take a look at my girl."

Don Fulgencio took one look, and his eyes started to well up.

"They're right. Your Mama Mayet should have been here to see you. You're so beautiful, *Hija*." He took Imelda's hands and squeezed them with both his hands.

"*Tio* Fule, it's time," Gloria said as she handed him the bridal veil. "I fastened the *peineta* of Tia Mayet to the veil. That way, the veil will be more secure."

Don Fulgencio took the hair comb and veil, and with Gloria's help, he placed it over Imelda's head and covered her face in the process. Gloria fastened the hair comb with a couple of hairpins.

"Time to take you to the church," Don Fulgencio declared as he extended his arm to Imelda.

The two started to walk down the stairs. At the bottom, before the foyer, there was a portrait of Imelda's mom. They stopped by the painting of Doña Marietta. Gloria handed over a small bouquet of flowers to Imelda. She promptly placed it on a vase on the table directly beneath her mother's picture. She then blew a kiss towards Doña Marietta's image.

Holding on to her father's arm, they proceeded to walk through the front door. Gloria and *Yaya* Pacing followed them to the courtyard. There, a *kalesa* was waiting for them. Don Fulgencio helped Imelda into the *kalesa* before taking a seat for himself. Gloria and *Yaya* Pacing took the next *kalesa*.

Don Fulgencio noticed Imelda being quiet and looking very pensive. "What's the matter, Imelda," asked Don Fulgencio, "Are you nervous?"

'No, Papa," she answered quickly.

Imelda was actually thinking of Kenji and the last time they saw each other…

Imelda was sitting at the veranda reading a book when Don Fulgencio came up from behind her.

"Imelda, honey, guess who is here?" asked Don Fulgencio as he leaned over to get a kiss on the check from Imelda.

She saw Kenji was behind her papa. His face was almost in a grimace.

"I think you remember Kenji. I introduced him to you a few months ago," said Don Fulgencio as he took a seat next to Imelda.

Imelda and Kenji both nodded at each other in acknowledgment. Imelda was worried about what was about to happen. He never mentioned that he was going to come by today. He seemed very serious.

"I came to let you know that I have been called back to Japan this morning. I will be leaving in a few hours," Kenji explained.

Imelda was surprised! This announcement was so unexpected. "What is he going to say now?" she asked herself.

Kenji faced Don Fulgencio and took a deep breath before continuing, "I wanted to ask your permission to…"

"Oh no!" Imelda thought to herself as she gasped. With her eyes looking directly at Kenji, she said a silent, *"No."* Fortunately, Don Fulgencio had his back towards her, so he did not see Imelda signaling Kenji.

"…to discuss our continued business dealings when I get back," Kenji said as he nodded to Imelda that he understood.

"Oh, Kenji. You need not worry. You are most welcome here

anytime," replied Don Fulgencio as he brought out his cigar. He took a whiff of it before taking out his cigar clippers. Don Fulgencio snipped his cigar and proceeded to light it up.

"If Imelda is interested, I would like to give her some riding pointers as you had asked," Kenji offered.

"That's a good idea," Don Fulgencio said as he turned to Imelda. "You better take him up on his offer. I have to go to City Hall to take care of another matter. It seems Ignacio's son, Eddie is in trouble again, and I told Ignacio that I would help him."

Imelda stood up to give her papa a kiss. Don Fulgencio turned to Kenji and shook his hand. "Have a safe trip," he said and then promptly left the veranda.

"Imelda, I was going to talk to your father about us," Kenji said in disdain. "I would like to take you to Japan with me."

Imelda was startled by this announcement. She would want nothing more than to be with Kenji. The idea that they would be apart is heartbreaking. But then the thought of leaving her Papa was simply unthinkable.

"Kenji, I cannot leave my Papa," she painfully said. "I will wait for your return."

Kenji made a move to get closer to Imelda, but she shifted away from him while looking around to check if there was anyone around. No one really knew about them. Being seen together publicly is something they avoided.

"Imelda, I do not know when I will be back," Kenji said solemnly as he took her hand. "And my life is there. I have an accomplished career there. I'm not young enough to start over here."

They both sat there in silence. One would say it was quiet between Kenji and Imelda for a long time. Both considered what to say next, but both knew they were at an impasse. His leaving could be it; the one moment that would define their relationship.

"I have to take care of Papa. I am all that he has. I cannot leave him," answered Imelda with her eyes looking at the ground away from Kenji.

"So that is it then," Kenji said utterly resigned.

The *kalesa* wheel rolled over a pebble that caused it to jerk slightly, pulling Imelda out from her reverie. Imelda saw the cathedral as the *kalesa* came around the corner. She recognized some of the people milling about the front of the church, smiling and waving as they pulled up. They were there for her wedding. Don Fulgencio was busy waving back and thanking them for coming. He alighted from the *kalesa* then proceeded to help Imelda.

Gloria and *Yaya* Pacing followed to make sure Imelda's dress and veil were in place. The four slowly joined the rest of the wedding party.

As Imelda took her papa's arm, she took a deep breath and began to walk down the aisle. She saw neighbors, relatives, and friends line the aisle; all in big smiles as she passed them. There he stood at the altar waiting for her with his stupid grin. But closer, Ryan was actually tearing up.

Don Fulgencio gave Imelda a hug and a kiss before handing her over to Ryan. Imelda's papa suddenly felt so sad. He thought to himself, she is getting married, and I won't see her sweet face as often as I would like. Imelda is all grown up." He said to himself in deep sorrow, "My baby is leaving me."

Ryan was overwhelmed when he saw Imelda because she was quite the vision of beauty. He couldn't help himself. His heart leaped for joy when he saw her. *"I can't believe I am marrying her,"* he thought to himself. Thanks to Don Fulgencio, he made it all happen a few months ago…

"Let's all raise a glass to Don Fulgencio! May he have many more joyous years to come," cheered Dr. Jose as he finished his birthday speech. Everyone in the room cheered and clapped for Don Fulgencio's birthday.

His party was a huge celebration as evidenced by practically having the whole town at his hacienda. There were tables and chairs scattered on the property.

Each table was covered with a beautiful, heavily embroidered tablecloth and lit with a lantern. The same material covered the chairs to match the tables. The table setting is with porcelain plates and actual silverware. It included vases of gladiolas and orchids.

There were servers running around serving drinks and busing tables. Even the trees had lanterns hanging from their limbs. A group of men to the side of the dance floor played live music. Clearly, Don Fulgencio did not spare any expense!

"Is there anyone else who would like to say something?" asked the host of the program.

"I would like to say a few words," volunteered Ryan as he got up from his seat and walked towards the middle of the dance floor.

He took the microphone and started to say, "Don Fulgencio, everyone here knows what a gracious and benevolent person you are. You are the one anyone in this town would turn to for help or advice.

Your generosity knows no bounds. Your wisdom is highly sought after. May you have continued health and happiness always. Cheers!" He then raised his glass of whiskey and took a big sip.

Everyone followed Ryan's cue and raised their glasses for Don Fulgencio.

Ryan then hurriedly announced, "I also want to take this great occasion to say something that I have felt for a very long time." He walked to the table where Don Fulgencio was seated together with Imelda and Gloria.

"Don Fulgencio, you have been so kind to me all these months. I have fallen deeply in love with your daughter, Imelda. I would like to ask you for your permission to marry her," Ryan sincerely asked Don Fulgencio.

"Oh, Ryan," exclaimed Don Fulgencio, "I thought you would never ask!" He stood up and hugged Ryan. He took Ryan's hand, and then, he pulled Imelda to her feet, reached out for her hand and put their hands together.

Everyone stood up and clapped.

Ryan pulled out a tiny box from his pocket and opened it to reveal a beautiful engagement ring. He got down on one knee and presented the ring.

"Imelda, will you marry me?" he asked solemnly.

Imelda was shocked! Everyone was waiting for her answer.

"What would I say? Can I say no?" she thought to herself. Most likely not! If she did, she would embarrass both her Papa and Ryan, especially after what Don Fulgencio did. Imelda felt so much pressure. She felt time slowing down with a million things running through her

head at the speed of light. People seemed frozen in time, all waiting for her answer. What is she to do?

"Yes," Imelda answered and time seemed to speed back up again and caught up with the present. People cheered and clapped. Drinks were being poured and consumed rapidly.

The merriment went to another level as the birthday party was now an engagement party.

The wedding celebration was even more significant than Don Fulgencio's birthday party was. Expecting to feed the whole town, Imelda's household cooked for days. There was not just one roast pig, but several and the best seafood was on the menu. All the fiesta fare food was available in abundance. Yes, there was enough food for everyone and then some.

Food was not the only thing in great supply. There were flowers everywhere! Ryan made sure that orchids from his plantation were flown in for the wedding. Imelda's bouquet was enormous and trailed on the ground. There were also local flowers, and many of them were sweet-smelling. They were a combination of Ylang-ylang, Magnolia, varieties of orchids: Vanda, Cattleyas and Phalaenopsis, and *Sampaguita*.

The celebration was disturbed by a commotion coming from the area where pigs were being roasted. The flames on one stake suddenly turned into a conflagration and it engulfed the entire pig and Danilo, *Yaya* Pacing's son, who was roasting the pig. He began running haphazardly until Eddie pushed him down and made him roll on the ground to extinguish the fire. Both Eddie and Danilo were screaming. Eddie began profusely apologizing to the Danilo.

Soon after, Dr. Jose came and started to help. He immediately took charge of the situation and gave instructions to others to bring Danilo to his clinic.

Don Fulgencio and *Yaya* Pacing, who were running, were soon at the scene as well.

"What happened?" Don Fulgencio asked while catching his breath.

Eddie answered, "It's my fault, Don Fulgencio. I accidentally dropped my bottle of *lambanog* when I bumped into Danilo. Some of it must have gotten on Danilo and the hot coals. I'm so sorry." He was so apologetic in his tone and stance.

Yaya Pacing started yelling at him, "You're drunk again! Look at what you did to my Danilo!"

Dr. Jose held *Yaya* Pacing by her shoulders and said, "Pacing, let's go. Danilo needs our attention." He tried his best to pull her away from Eddie.

Yaya Pacing broke free and slapped Eddie. She screamed at him, "You are nothing but a useless drunk. If my Danilo dies, I will kill you myself!" Her threat stung Eddie like a knife stab!

Dr. Jose managed to get ahold of *Yaya* Pacing again and gently pulled her in the direction of his clinic. Two men came over and escorted her to Danilo.

Ignacio arrived just as *Yaya* Pacing was walking away. She yelled at him, "Look at what your son did!" She was so grief-stricken; tears were rolling down her face in torrents.

Don Fulgencio asked Dr. Jose, "Will Danilo be okay?"

The doctor turned to face him and said, "It does not look good. He has major burns all over his body. It will be a miracle if he makes it at all. I have to go."

Dr. Jose hurried to catch up with *Yaya* Pacing and the others.

Eddie was swaying as he stood in front of Don Fulgencio. He was visibly drunk. The smell of alcohol emanates from him.

Ignacio was upset. He punched Eddie in the abdomen. "*Anak*, how could you?" he shouted. "I told you to stop drinking!"

"*Itay*, it was an accident. I did not mean to harm Danilo." Eddie tried to explain as he clutched his stomach and tried to stand up straight.

"Eddie," Don Fulgencio started to say. "I told you that you should stop drinking when I bailed you out of jail. I do not know how else to help you."

"You are dead to me!" exclaimed Ignacio. "You are nothing but an embarrassment! I'm glad your *Nanay* is not here to see this, or it would have broken her heart." He turned his back away from Eddie.

"*Itay*, I'm sorry. I never meant for this to happen!" pleaded Eddie as he fell on his knees, trying to hold on to Ignacio's feet.

"You have to leave the property. Go pack your bags and never come back," instructed Don Fulgencio angrily.

As Don Fulgencio was admonishing Eddie, another commotion started in the main house. Don Fulgencio quickly made his way back. At that point, someone was rigging the microphone to the radio so that everyone could hear the news.

"Pearl Harbor was attacked by the Japanese! It has been completely destroyed. Numerous casualties!" the announcer on the radio said.

A number of the guests quickly left. A few lingered to continue to listen to the breaking news. Some women were crying into their handkerchiefs while men were smoking their cigars. Only Don Fulgencio noticed Ryan walk into the room. He had already changed out of his wedding attire. He crouched down to where Don Fulgencio was seated.

Ryan then said, "I have to leave for Hawaii now, Papa. I must check on my plantation and my people there. My Dad left the land to me, and I have since taken care of the people living there. I must fly out now."

"I cannot let you take Imelda with you. What if the Japanese are still there? It will not be safe for her to go with you," Don Fulgencio told Ryan. There was no way that he would allow it.

"I understand, Sir, and I also agree. Imelda will be much safer here with you," Ryan concurred. "I will come back as soon as I secure the plantation and all its residents."

"I will take care of Imelda," Don Fulgencio assured him. "She will be safe and well attended to."

At that moment, Imelda walked into the room. She has changed out of her wedding gown as well. She was making her way to her papa when she noticed that both Don Fulgencio and Ryan were talking intently. From the looks of their faces, she surmised that it must be something serious.

"Papa," Imelda called out as she made her way to them.

"*Hija*," answered Don Fulgencio as he reached out for her and gently directed her to the seat next to him.

"Imelda, I have to leave for Hawaii right away," stated Ryan. "I want more than anything to take you with me, but I am afraid that it may not be safe for you."

Ryan held both Imelda's hands and continued, "Your Papa will make sure you are safe until I return."

"But aren't the Japanese shooting everything down? Both ships and planes! It's not safe for you, either!" exclaimed Imelda. In spite of how she truly felt about Ryan, she genuinely did care for his safety. He may act like a pompous ass sometimes but she cannot imagine him getting hurt.

"I will be okay, Imelda. Don't worry. I am an experienced pilot, and I do know my way around," Ryan assured her as he hugged her.

"Now I have to go," he said and kissed her forehead. "I love you."

FALSE HEROES

Crash! The door of the basement came crashing down. Japanese soldiers were quickly and surely breaking down the door! They were shouting very animatedly.

Everyone in the basement froze. Quickly, *Yaya* Pacing extinguished the small lantern light. There was nowhere else to hide! Both Imelda and Gloria clung to each other. *Yaya* Pacing went to their side to stand by them. Dr. Jose and Ignacio were standing at the other end. Everyone was holding their breath in a futile attempt not to be heard.

Finally, the Japanese soldiers were able to break down the barricaded door. Beams of sunlight pierced the darkened room. Consequently, rapid gunshots rang out.

Everyone braced themselves with bated breath. Tears were running down their faces, and yet they did not dare make a sound. *"This is it,"* everyone was thinking to themselves.

A Japanese soldier entered the room. Another soldier followed him in and then another! Menacingly, they brandished their bayonets. Seeing the people inside the basement, the soldiers pointed their guns at them and shouted for them to go outside.

One by one, they went out of the basement. The occupants of the cellar shielded their eyes as they came out into the sunlight. They were all pale and visibly malnourished. Standing up straight was not easy after being bent over for a couple of months.

None of them dared to go out after they buried Don Fulgencio. Ignacio and Dr. Jose dug the hole while the women wrapped Don Fulgencio's body in blankets. Gently, they lowered his remains into the ground. They all wanted to pray and linger, but they understood that it was not safe. As they hurriedly went back to hiding, Imelda and Gloria's tears fell in torrents. Don Fulgencio deserves a proper funeral, but this will have to do in the interim.

Now the Japanese soldiers were brandishing their weapons again. They pushed and shouted at the captives to line up against the wall. As their eyes adjusted to the light, that was when they saw the traitor, the *Makapili*.

He stood there with a *bayong* over his head with holes cut out for the eyes. He walked from one end of the line to the other. The *Makapili* finally stopped and pointed his dreaded finger at *Yaya* Pacing.

Both Imelda and Gloria clung tightly to *Yaya* Pacing as the Japanese soldiers pulled her out of the line-up. The soldiers forcibly pushed the younger women back into the line.

Yaya Pacing stood there defiantly, fiercely wiping the tears running down her face and looked at the *Makapili* square in the face.

"I am not afraid of you!" she bravely told him, yet she trembled visibly.

The *Makapili* openly laughed, and his laughter caused Ignacio's ears to perk up. *"I know that laugh,"* Ignacio thought.

He quickly stood by *Yaya* Pacing and shouted at the *Makapili*, "Eddie, is that you?!"

The soldiers were about to push Ignacio back into the line, but the *Makapili* stopped laughing and waved his hand to stop them.

He then started to pace between *Yaya* Pacing and Ignacio.

"Eddie, I know it is you!" Ignacio declared as he recognized the pair of eyes behind the *bayong*.

The *Makapili* took off the *bayong* from his head and revealed himself. It was indeed Eddie.

"What are you trying to do, *Anak*?" asked Ignacio in bewilderment. He was deeply upset that his own son had betrayed him and shown the Japanese soldiers their hideout.

"*Anak*?!" Eddie retorted. "The last time I saw you, you disowned me!"

Eddie was fuming! *"Really? After everything that happened at Imelda's wedding, you will still call me son?"* he thought to himself.

"Eddie, stop this nonsense!" shouted Dr. Jose trying to diffuse the situation.

"Hmm. You all think you are better than me?" Eddie exclaimed mockingly. "The Japanese believed in me. They listen to me. I am important to them. You? You are nothing!" Eddie shouted at them. He was strutting around to show his importance. He wanted recognition and fear from everyone.

"So, you think you are some bigshot? You are nothing and will always be nothing!" rebuked *Yaya* Pacing.

Eddie immediately slapped *Yaya* Pacing so hard that blood pooled at the corner of her mouth.

Ignacio lurched over to grab Eddie but the Japanese soldier sprang into action and stabbed him before he could even touch him. Ignacio fell to the ground and started bleeding profusely.

"*Itay!*" screamed Eddie as he got down on his knees to be near his father.

Ignacio could only manage to look at Eddie as tears rolled down his cheek. His eyes turned glassy and his limbs went limp.

Eddie was so enraged! In his fury, he grabbed a rifle from a soldier standing nearby and started shooting randomly. His shots hit Dr. Jose and *Yaya* Pacing. He shot others in the line-up as well but stopped short at Imelda and Gloria.

He looked at both of them and said, "Oh, I will get paid a lot for both of you." In his mind, he knew what to do with them; he is going to get rewarded handsomely.

Gloria and Imelda were holding hands crying over the loss of *Yaya* Pacing, Ignacio, and Dr. Jose. They wanted to get to them but the soldiers did not let them. Plus, Eddie still had this crazed look on him. He did not only look detestable but nearly insane!

The long march began. The women were fearful for each other's safety. The Japanese soldier behind them kept pushing them forward as they walked towards the commandant's residence.

Eddie was holding a bottle of *lambanog* as he walked in front of this pitiful parade of captives. He took long sips as they walked. It was very evident that what transpired earlier was never expected. He was dazed and got so drunk. His *bayong* was in one hand while his *lambanog* was on the other and he walked with a swagger. He had captives and, he was sure, the payment and recognition would be lavish. As they neared the commandant's residence, he quickly put his *lambanog* inside his *bayong* and tried to tidy himself up.

Gloria and Imelda were brought to a room where the windows were nailed shut. When the door closed behind them, they tried to open it again, but it was locked.

The door reopened later and one Japanese soldier went in while another guarded the entrance. The one inside was definitely deciding who to choose between the two women. He was walking towards Imelda when Gloria decidedly stood between them. He shrugged and pulled Gloria towards him. The soldier inspected her like she was a cow. He held her chin and looked at both sides of her face. He ran his hands down her breast, straight down her belly to her crotch, and over her hips. He then took her out of the room while Imelda desperately tried to hold on to her.

Both women cried and fiercely held on to each other as much as they could but another soldier pulled Imelda off and shoved her back into the room. He quickly locked the door behind him.

Imelda heard Gloria screaming and crying in the next room. She could hear thumping sounds emanating from the wall between them. Imelda sat by the wall with her hands on it, crying. If only she can go through the wall and help Gloria. She pressed herself unto the wall in tears and felt so powerless.

Gloria was pushed, pulled, and clawed by several soldiers in the room next to Imelda. They tore off her clothing and rubbed their hands, faces, and crotch all over her. Some were half-dressed while others were completely naked. They were groping her, slapping her and pulling her in every direction. Gloria felt a few of them bite her hard while others punched her. She was helplessly violated and assaulted. The soldiers were worse than animals! Savagely and inhumanely, they had their way with her.

Gloria wished and prayed hard to get away from this until she eventually gave up and passed out.

Imelda waited by the door. She was ready to pounce on the guard as soon as it opened. She planned to attack the guard, run out, and look for Gloria but when the door finally opened, she was unable to carry out her plan. The soldiers opened the door and in they dragged Gloria's seemingly lifeless body.

Imelda screamed when she saw Gloria. She ran to her to make sure she was still alive. Gloria was black and blue everywhere. Her clothing was so shredded it barely covered her. There were blood on her lips, ears, nose, everywhere – but she was alive. Imelda held her and rocked her gently, crying softly.

After what seemed like an eternity, Gloria's eyes slowly opened. She immediately felt the pain radiating all over her body. She could barely move. She was on Imelda's lap, who had fallen asleep while cradling her. She carefully rolled off Imelda's lap so as not to wake her but Imelda woke up anyhow and tried to pull Gloria back to her in an embrace. Gloria winced in pain and cried.

Imelda felt helpless. She wanted to help Gloria but could not. What is there that she can offer to alleviate Gloria's pain? Nothing. Imelda could only carefully help Gloria to sit up.

The door opened again and this time another soldier pulled

Imelda by the hair and dragged her out of the room. Gloria tried to pull her back but she was too weak to do anything. Imelda tried desperately to fight back by kicking and screaming. She struggled to free herself by flailing her arms desperately to punch her attacker.

The soldier put her in the next room where other soldiers were already waiting. A few of them were already undressed! They immediately made a circle around Imelda and tried to grab her while she fought back. They mocked her and toyed with her as if she was some trapped animal. Eventually, one soldier managed to pull her off her feet and pinned her down while the others gathered around. Imelda was kicking as much as she could. She did this with her eyes blurred with tears as she made every effort to push and kick them away. Then, unexpectedly, someone yanked the man on top of her and the rest backed away.

Imelda was ready to punch anyone that came close to her when she heard a familiar voice. "You're safe now," the voice said calmly.

Hearing the voice, she looked past her tears and discovered it was Kenji! He leaned forward to pull her up, but before he could, she already jumped into his arms. She started to cry, uncontrollably! He carried her out of the room and brought her to another room where Gloria was already waiting.

Kenji set her down next to Gloria. The cousins, both in tears, clung to each other tightly. He turned around and ordered the soldier standing guard to get food and clothing for the women.

Kenji knelt on one knee next to them, his head bowed, and said, "I'm sorry this happened to you. But you are safe now, and I will take care of you."

Imelda, still surprised, looked at him and asked, "How is it that you are here?"

IMELDA

1940s

"When I heard that the Imperial Japanese Army occupied Lipa, I asked for this assignment and tried to come as soon as I could," Kenji explained.

"I even went to your home but you had already abandoned it. I looked for you everywhere. When I heard a *Makapili* brought in two women from your town, I did my best to get here quickly," Kenji continued.

"But how can you do all this?" asked Imelda.

"I am a colonel. I am actually in command here," Kenji stated.

Soldiers came into the room and brought a table, a few chairs, and clothing. The food arrived quickly soon after. They left the room after setting it up.

Imelda looked at the table, then she looked at Kenji as if to ask permission to eat. He nodded and she quickly sat at the table and started eating. Kenji helped Gloria to the table, so she too could eat.

He sat next to them and watched them eat. "Slow down. There's more from where it came from."

But it didn't matter. Gloria and Imelda hardly had anything to eat since the war broke out. They were famished. They quickly gobbled up everything on the table. They fed themselves using their hands with as much food as they could put in their mouths. They finished everything on the table.

Kenji had beds brought into the room after their meal and soon Gloria was sound asleep.

Imelda sat next to Gloria. She held her hand while tears slowly fell from her face. So much has happened, she thought. *Yaya* Pacing and Ignacio are dead, Eddie is a *Makapili*, Gloria was raped, Kenji's rescue.

93

It was all a nightmare! She would not know what to do if Gloria died.

There was a soft knock. Imelda opened the door to find Kenji outside. He saw Gloria was asleep, so he motioned for Imelda to follow him. She gently closed the door behind her and followed Kenji to another room.

As soon as Kenji closed the door, Imelda rushed to embrace him. Then she started to cry softly on his shoulder. He held her gently and began to sway. "It is going to be alright, Imelda. I'm here for you," he said tenderly. Kenji had his arms securely around her to reassure her that she was now safe; that he was there for her and she no longer had to worry.

The sultry evening was finally cooling down. The single window in the room was open. It let a refreshing breeze in as the lace curtains gently danced with it. The smell of *Sampaguita* wafted into the room. Outside, cicadas were singing.

She looked up at him with tears brimming in her eyes. Kenji brushed the strands of hair away from her face as he tenderly and lovingly looked at her. Their eyes locked. That intangible connection was there and it was more profound than either of them had expected.

Their parted lips slowly found each other. They touched softly at first. Kenji wanted to be gentle as though to reassure her. As their lips parted, they looked at each other more intently. Then Imelda pressed on with more passion.

Soon they were quickly taking off their clothes and began to make love as the cicadas outside continued to sing. Neither of them heard the cicadas as they passionately held on to each other. The male cicada called out to its mate in song. It was loud and filled the night air. A call for intimacy, compassion, and love.

LOOK WHO IS COMING FOR DINNER

"Honey," exclaimed Ryan on his way towards the kitchen.

"Yes?" Imelda responded but she did not look up because she was in the middle of cutting some vegetables.

"Our Hawaiian plantation is now sold!" Ryan announced.

"Huh? I did not even know that we were selling it," Imelda remarked, not hiding her surprise. "I thought you wanted to keep it for Adele," she continued as she reached for the onions.

"Well," Ryan replied. "That property is huge. Not sure if Adele would like to keep it. Plus, I got an offer that I cannot refuse. The buyer is paying cash and well above the market rate. I can buy a smaller lot for Adele if she really wants one."

"Oh, I see. That is great then!" said Imelda, who was now cutting an eggplant. "Good luck with that."

"What do you mean by that?" Ryan asked as he moved closer to her.

Imelda put down the knife, removed the string beans from the colander, quickly shook the excess water off the beans before placing them on the cutting board and started to cut them. "Just a few days ago, you told me there were a lot of Japanese nationals buying property in Hawaii. We might not get another chance to own property if land prices keep going up."

"True, but heck, the money is so good! I can definitely afford to get something for Adele as soon as the money comes in," Ryan explained excitedly.

"Well then, I guess it's final. It's a win-win," Imelda said as she checked on the tenderness of the meat.

"Happy you feel that way," Ryan said as he looked about the kitchen. "The buyer asked to meet the family, so I invited him for dinner tonight. Adele, Kent, and the twins are coming too. I called them already," he announced.

Imelda stopped cutting and looked up at Ryan.

"Tonight? Do we really have to? Isn't it such a short notice? I do not think I cooked enough. Maybe we should simply go out for dinner?" Imelda suggested.

"Nah. The buyer was pretty adamant about coming to dinner at our home. So, I said ok," said Ryan matter-of-factly.

"Sounds pushy," Imelda said as she started to fry the onions she had chopped earlier.

"Come on. He is buying the plantation. The least we can do is give him dinner. If it helps, I can order more food and have it delivered here," he offered.

"Well, I hope he likes Filipino food because that is what I am making," said Imelda as she continued chopping vegetables vigorously.

"Actually, there is something about this guy," Ryan said as he leaned over the counter.

"What do you mean?" asked Imelda as she checked on her pot and stirred its contents. "If you think he is not trustworthy, why invite him to our home?"

"No. It is not that," answered Ryan as he put a spoon into the pot to taste the food. "I cannot put my finger on it just yet."

Imelda scanned the kitchen to see if she has enough ingredients to make more food. She opened the refrigerator and took out more vegetables and meat to cook. Taking stock of what she had on the kitchen countertop, she slowly nodded, assured that they will have enough food for dinner.

"Well, figure it out quickly before letting him in. I do not want trouble," Imelda finally replied as she started to stir-fry the meat.

"I'm sure he is alright. I just have this weird feeling I've met him before," Ryan said while waving his spoon.

The doorbell chimed; Ryan opened the door to find his daughter, Adele, her cousin, Kent, and his twins, Margaux and Johann.

"Hi Grandpa," the twins rushed to give Ryan a peck on the check.

"Well, hello there," Ryan said as he hugged his grandkids.

"Hi, Dad! I ran into Kent and the twins as I was walking up the driveway," Adele said, holding a bunch of tulips. "I think mom will like this!"

"Wonderful," Ryan exclaimed in relief. "She was a little annoyed that I didn't get any flowers for the table."

"Uhm, yea. She called me earlier just for that," Adele said with a grin on her face.

"Well, you know where the vases are. Go ahead and put them in water. I think your mom is about done setting the table."

"Hi, Uncle Ryan," said Kent as he gave him a quick hug. "I, too, brought something. Here are a few bottles of wine. I heard we are celebrating tonight. Mary Ann sends her regrets because she is still in the East Coast. Something came up at work, so she had to delay her flight home," Kent explained.

"Thank you. No problem. Come on in. You can put the wine in the bar. You know your way around," Ryan said as they walked into the foyer.

"Barry and Bruce can't join us either. I guess whatever my brother did, they are charging Bruce, so he will be staying in jail 'til Barry can post bail. Barry is busy trying to do just that. I think he should just leave Bruce to rot in jail." Kent said bluntly, talking about his brother and stepfather.

Ryan paused and looked at Kent. "Does Diego know?" Ryan asked.

"Diego, that bastard of a father, never did anything. What makes you think he will do something now? Since he threw us out, he has never lifted a finger for Bruce or me. He said mom is nothing but garbage. Mom had to raise us single-handedly. He may be our biological father but he is nothing to us. Barry has done more for us," Kent replied.

Ryan tapped Kent's shoulder and said, "It's going to be ok. Let's not think of that right now and enjoy dinner. Okay?"

Kent and the twins were busy taking off their coats and Ryan was helping to hang them in the hallway closet when the doorbell chimed again.

Imelda saw they were all busy doing something, so she yelled, "I'll get it!"

She opened the door and she gasped.

"Good evening, Imelda," the visitor calmly greeted her.

"You're here!" Imelda could barely speak as she froze in place.

"You are, too!" Kenji replied with a big smile. They both stood there, looking at each other. Neither knew what to do next. Should they hug, should they shake hands? A very awkward silence ensued.

"Hey, Kenji," Ryan exclaimed as he walked towards the door. He extended his hand to Kenji for a handshake then proceeded to pull him past Imelda into the foyer.

"Let me take your coat," he said to Kenji as he started to open the door to the coat closet to get a hanger.

Imelda walked towards both men. Ryan introduced her to Kenji. "I see you've met my wife, Imelda."

"How do you do," Kenji said as he bowed toward her.

"Honey, this is Kenji. He bought our plantation in Hawaii," Ryan said. "Let me call the rest of the gang," Ryan announced as he motioned for Adele and Kent to join them.

"Adele, this is Kenji. Kenji, this is my daughter Adele," Ryan said. "And this is Kent, my nephew, Adele's cousin."

Kenji was speechless when he saw Adele. She was the spitting image of Imelda when she was younger. Totally caught unprepared, he didn't know what to say. "Actually, I have met your grandfather, Don Fulgencio. He was a truly kind man."

Ryan's eyes widened as if he finally solved a riddle.

"That's it!" exclaimed Ryan. "I knew there was something familiar about you. You're that guy he mentioned who was part of the Japanese Olympic delegation. No wonder you looked familiar. I think we did meet briefly, when I sold my horse to him. Small world!"

"That's right," Kenji confirmed. "If I remember correctly, your plantation is full of wonderful orchids."

"Well, it is yours now," answered Ryan.

Imelda thought she was going to pass out. Kenji was her big secret! No one in her family can know about Kenji and her past, and here he is giving out information voluntarily. She had to do something quickly.

Imelda nudged the side table just enough for the vase to tip over. Adele immediately ran over to catch the vase before it rolled off the table. Imelda excused herself to get a towel to wipe up the water that had spilled.

"Sorry, I am a bit clumsy ever since I was hospitalized a few years ago," she said when she returned and began to wipe the table.

There was only silence.

Concern registered on Kenji's face. He was about to say something but decided not to. He was worried that in doing so, it might upset Imelda more.

"Well, let's all go into the dining room. Imelda prepared a great Filipino meal," Ryan broke the silence as he directed everyone to the adjoining room.

Adele helped Imelda set up the dinner table while Kent tried to get the twins to stay seated.

"You have quite a beautiful dinner table setting," Kenji commented as he marveled at it.

"Thank you. Imelda is great at decorating and putting things together," answered Ryan.

"Actually, it was Kent's mom, *Ninang* Gloria, who puts everything together like a designer. She has an eye for really nice things, and so when she and mom go shopping, even if they meant to pick up only one thing, they come home with sets of this and that," Adele revealed.

"Yup, that's mom, alright," Kent agreed. "For such a petite woman, she can haul a bunch of stuff like a longshoreman."

"Kent, don't talk about your mom like that," Imelda stopped her nephew. "She doesn't buy nonsense stuff. It's almost like an ideology, a philosophy, a way of life for art," she explained.

"It's too bad you missed her. She would have been excited to see someone from the good old days," Ryan remarked.

"May I ask where Gloria is?" inquired Kenji as he cautiously looked at Imelda.

"Mom is in the hospital," Kent answered quickly.

"Sorry to hear that," replied Kenji. "Will she be alright? Nothing serious, I hope."

"Mom is not doing well; I am afraid to say," Kent replied rather reluctantly as he helped Johann cut his meat. "She is frail," he continued.

"*Ninang* Gloria is a powerful, beautiful, and independent woman," Adele declared. "In fact, she is helping me advocate for the comfort women who were victims of the Japanese occupation of the Philippines. She is not weak in any sense of the word."

"Adele, that's enough!" Imelda said firmly. "We are here to celebrate the sale of our plantation and not discuss the Japanese occupation."

"But Mama, the comfort women are getting old, and a few of them have already died or are dying. We need to gather all of them now before it is too late to advocate for each other so we can push for a formal apology from the Japanese."

"Now, you are going to insult our guest," Imelda said admonishing her daughter.

"Grandma, what are comfort women?" Margaux interjected in her tiny little voice.

Everyone at the dinner table fell silent and nervously looked at each other. Johann saw that the adults were exchanging glances and thought it was a game. He started to squeal in laughter.

"Margaux, comfort women are victims of war," Adele finally relented and explained.

"What are victims?" Margaux asked more.

"Honey, just please stop," Imelda said firmly, looking at Adele square in the face.

She turned to look at Margaux, "It is when bad things happen to people."

Before Margaux could ask another question, Imelda took Margaux's spoon and said, "We should talk about something else. Your food is getting cold. Here, let me help you with that."

"So, Kenji, do you still ride horses?" asked Ryan, hoping to change the conversation.

"Not as often as I would like. Since my stroke, I could not handle the hard and long rides anymore," Kenji explained.

Imelda looked up to check Kenji out. *"Is that why he stammers now? No wonder I am having difficulty understanding him,"* she thought to herself.

"Oh, that's a shame," replied Ryan. "But, isn't riding therapeutic though?"

"Ryan, I'm sure he has explored that avenue," Imelda interrupted.

"It's alright," Kenji replied as he looked at Ryan. "I actually have a ranch that caters to special needs children. Riding does wonders for riders of any age and needs."

"I want to ride a horse!" exclaimed Johann as he jumped up from his seat.

Kenji smiled as he looked at Johann, "Then you can come to my ranch and ride any horse as much as you would like."

"I want to ride a horse, too!" exclaimed Margaux eagerly.

"You can also come anytime, as long as it is alright with your parents," Kenji told Margaux with a big smile.

The rest of the dinner was uneventful save for the twin's antics. Johann managed to pour his whole glass of juice onto himself. Kent was about to stand up and take care of Johann when Imelda waved him off.

She excused herself and tugged on Johann to follow so that she could clean him up.

In the other room, Imelda hurriedly wiped Johann clean. While crouching in front of him, she selected a new shirt from his day bag and slipped it over his head.

"You look very ugly," Johann said while looking up past Imelda.

Imelda shushed Johann, "You are never to say something like that! Go and say, you're sorry."

She turned around and found Kenji standing behind her. He offered his hand and gently helped Imelda to her feet. The electricity between them was intense as they touched each other.

The tension was only broken when Johann exclaimed, "I'm sorry," before he ran away.

"Please meet me at the Conservatory of Flowers at five o'clock tomorrow," Kenji whispered into Imelda's ear just as she was about to chase after Johann.

Kenji returned from the bathroom to see that everyone had moved to the living room. Imelda and Adele were in a heated discussion.

"Mom, you were there during the Japanese occupation. I am sure you know of the atrocities of the Japanese. We only want you to help us. Help the women. Help me give them a voice. We should all stand up for them. Who else will support them?" asked Adele.

"The Japanese reparation should be enough. The Filipinas have suffered enough. Why spend their remaining time being dragged through the mud again? They need to be left alone in peace. Nothing good will come of it. The past is the past. Let it die there," exclaimed Imelda.

"Mom, you know very well that is not the point. The point is the Filipina comfort women want the Japanese to acknowledge what they have done and apologize. That is all they ever wanted," explained Adele.

Imelda let out a deep sigh. "We all want something, yet we all do not get what we want," she said.

"Oh, come on, Mom, you do not really believe that!" Adele chided her mom. "The Filipina comfort women deserve better! No woman should have to go through this. Being forced into sex slavery is an abomination! It is a large-scale rape of women conducted in an organized full-scale exploitation operation. It was a systematic abuse and trafficking of women as sex slaves. We are even considering joining forces with the women in China and Korea. We hope we can grow in numbers enough to push the issue."

"And there rests my bone of contention," said Imelda. "You are just pushing. Pushing older women to confess up to the pain they have suffered and made them relive every painful moment again and again. And to what end? Do you think you can really make a change?"

"Mama, trying is different from not doing anything at all," said Adele softly.

At that point, Kenji decided it was time to say his goodbye. He walked into the room and said, "Hello again, everyone. It is getting late, and I have an early morning. I had an excellent evening. Thank you, Ryan, and Imelda for the wonderful dinner."

"Oh, you do not have to go just yet. Stay awhile and let us have a drink," Ryan said.

Imelda was already by the hallway closet, pulling out Kenji's coat when he declined Ryan's offer to stay longer. "Thank you, but I do have an early morning meeting to attend to. Maybe some other time."

"It's good to see you. Have a safe trip home," Imelda told Kenji as she was handing him his coat.

"Well, then. I will just see you when the paperwork for the sale is done," Ryan said.

Kenji nodded and bowed to the family after Imelda opened the front door for him. As he passed Imelda, he whispered to her, "See you tomorrow."

Imelda quickly closed the door behind him as if she did not hear what he had just said.

Kenji turned around to catch another glimpse of Imelda but she had already closed the door. He sighed and walked away from the house.

Kenji was buttoning up his coat as he walked to his car. He pulled his gloves out of his pocket when a small box fell out of it. He stooped down to pick it up. Kenji opened the box to check that it was still there. In the box was the 15-carat blue diamond ring. He began to recall the day he acquired it...

He and Haruki were looking for Akito. The soldier posted outside told them that the colonel was in the house but was not sure specifically where. They looked in his office but it was empty before they finally found him eating in the dining room.

Eusebia was serving Akito lunch when both Haruki and Kenji approached them.

"Good. You are both here," said Akito as he looked up at them.

"We were summoned here. I thought General Yamashita would be here," Haruki said.

"Relax. Have a seat. Join me for lunch. We will get to General Yamashita soon enough. Eusebia is a good cook," Akito said as he motioned to Eusebia to set two more table settings for the colonels.

Haruki and Kenji looked at each other hesitating and considering what to do next.

"You should learn to relax. Nothing has changed much since we were in the officer academy together," Akito assured them.

Both Haruki and Kenji took a seat on opposite sides of Akito. Kenji was anxious as he looked around whereas Haruki seemed to have relaxed already.

Eusebia brought in the dishes and began to serve the colonels. She kept her head down and never said a word. As she silently served the colonels, Akito started to talk about General Yamashita.

"The general is not here, but we are tasked with an important job," explained Akito.

This alarmed both Haruki and Kenji. They both glanced at each other apprehensively. Both colonels considered stopping Akito from discussing General Yamashita in front of Eusebia.

Akito laughed as he saw the expression on their faces. "Eusebia is alright," he reassured the men. "Believe me. I have her under control and I can assure you she will not be a problem."

"Eusebia," Akito called out to her as he motioned her to come closer.

Eusebia nervously approached the men. When she was within arms-length of Akito, he suddenly raised his hand. She quickly covered her face and bowed her head, fearful and silently cringing.

"See what I mean?" Akito pointed out to the men while grinning.

"Let's get to the matter at hand," Haruki said as he was anxious to finish the meeting.

"As you know, General Yamashita has been tasked with managing a great treasure for our Prince Chichibu. The Americans are gaining ground here and we have to secure the treasure. I am entrusting both of you to help me devise a plan on how to do so as well as executing it," Akito exclaimed.

"That is a vital task," Haruki said with a huge smile on his face. "I know I can speak for Kenji and say we are quite honored to be part of this undertaking," he said as he bowed deeply.

Kenji nodded and a bowed in return. "For your services, Prince Chichibu has authorized me to give these to both of you," he said as he handed each of them a small box.

Kenji and Haruki opened their respective boxes. They both let out a gasp when they saw what was inside. The boxes were lined with a black velvet fabric and each contained a blue diamond. From the size of the stone, they thought it must have been at least 15-carats.

Haruki picked his diamond up and held it to the light. It was beautiful! The color was deep blue and it was clear of any impurities. It glistened against the light.

Eusebia could not help but look at the diamond as Haruki held it up. She would have kept looking had she did not notice that Akito was looking at her. She looked away and began to refill the water glasses with the pitcher she was holding before scurrying away into the kitchen.

"It is a very good size gem," Akito stated shifting his attention back to the men.

"Not to look at a gift horse in the mouth, but truly, is this even real?" Haruki bowed and asked Akito humbly.

"Yes, it is a real blue diamond. Our Prince Chichibu is very generous," Akito stated.

Kenji was about to say something but then held back. Akito saw this and asked, "What is on your mind, Kenji?"

Kenji took a breath before saying, "This is a splendid gem but may I ask where it came from?"

"Well, if you must know, it came from a mine in India. I was told that during Prince Chichibu's extensive stay in Europe, he came across these gems," Akito explained.

"So, if this is truly valuable, why give it to us? Surely, it should be with all of the prince's prize possessions," Hakuri said tentatively, still examining the piece.

"Ah, but the prince values the safety of his treasures here. That kind of undertaking deserves rich rewards, don't you think? What are a few gems compared to the value of a treasure that needs to be secured?" Akito tauntingly said.

"It's beautiful and much appreciated! As a humble colonel in our Emperor's Imperial Army, I would have done this endeavor for much less or nothing at all," exclaimed Haruki as he bowed deeply.

"It is the prince's intent to reward you handsomely for this vital task," remarked Akito.

Kenji immediately knew what he was going to do with the diamond. He was going to give it to Imelda. When all this madness is over, he will present it to her and all will be right with the world.

The colonel's attention was quickly drawn to the presence of a soldier by the doorway. Hakuri and Kenji both noticed this and hurriedly put away their gems. Akito motioned the soldier to come forward. The soldier marched in and then bowed towards Akito.

"What is it?" Akito asked not masking his impatience with the intrusion.

The soldier straightened up and announced, "Sir, a *Makapili* just brought in a prisoner. He claims that the captive is a member of the *Hukbalahap*. There is valuable information to be reaped from him. Some of the intel acquired is about the Americans. He said that a large American contingent is fast approaching."

Akito paused to digest the new information and consider his options.

"Do you have the current location of this contingent? How big is it? How heavily armed are they? What do they have on them, just rifles or something more?" Akito asked the soldier in succession.

"Sir, I do not have all of that information yet," he replied.

"Well, continue with the interrogation and come back when you have a more complete report to give to me!" he forcefully instructed and he dismissed the soldier.

Akito stood up to look at the map hanging on the wall.

"We will need to move soon and quickly," Akito declared while mapping out their next base.

HELLO, GUESS WHO

Imelda knocked softly at the door to Gloria's hospital room.

"Come in," Gloria called out.

Imelda was hardly past the curtains separating Gloria's bed from the other patient when she blurted out, "Gloria. I saw Kenji!"

"What?! When did this happen?" Gloria exclaimed.

Imelda held Gloria's hand. "I saw him last night. Ryan brought him over for dinner."

Gloria frowned and looked confused. "How did that happen? Does Ryan remember meeting him at your place in Lipa? Does Ryan even know about you and Kenji? That you were together?" she asked.

"Of course not!" exclaimed Imelda. "Ryan received an offer for his plantation in Hawaii that he couldn't refuse and it turns out Kenji is his buyer!"

"What?" exclaimed Gloria! "What a coincidence!"

"I don't think so," answered Imelda. "There are two other nearby plantations that are up for sale at a much lower price. Kenji knew he put a bid on Ryan's plantation and made that offer well over the market price. I am certain he wanted to make sure Ryan would take it."

"Oh," said Gloria. "Kenji did not say anything to Ryan, I hope."

"Other than knowing Papa, I do not think so," Imelda answered.

Gloria heaved a sigh of relief. "Then what is the problem? How come you look troubled?"

"Kenji asked me to meet him today," Imelda, looking worried, explained.

She started pacing about the hospital room. She knew she wanted to meet Kenji and yet she was afraid of what would transpire.

"Oh. That can be a problem!" exclaimed Gloria. "Does Ryan suspect anything? Will you go?" asked Gloria as she tried to sit up.

Imelda helped Gloria by fixing the pillows on her back.

"I want to," said Imelda softly as she looked away from her cousin.

"Then do it!" encouraged Gloria. "How is he? Does he still have that commanding stance of his?"

"No," answered Imelda. "He looks much older and different now. He said he had a stroke a few years back. You can hear that he is having some difficulty with his speech – he seems to be repeating himself. It's a bit weird. You know how he really does not talk much. It's like he is trying to assert himself."

"Oh!" Gloria exclaimed. "We are getting old. We are all not in the best of health. Me with my cancer, Ryan with his stroke, and you with your health scare a few years back."

Imelda looked at Gloria as she nodded in agreement.

"So, what will you do now?" asked Gloria.

"I do not know. A part of me wants to see Kenji, and another part wants him to go away," Imelda said in exasperation.

"Then you should go," said Gloria. "The last time we saw him, he said he was going to scout ahead to see if it was safe. But he never came back."

"It was during a thunderstorm, I remember," Imelda recalled. "I could not see very far at all that day because of the heavy downpour…"

The rain was falling so hard it caused the leaves and tree branches to bend. Except for the rain and the clap of thunder and lightning, one could not hear a thing. It was so difficult to see or hear anything but the torrential rain.

"There," exclaimed Kenji while pointing at what looked like a cave from a distance. "Let's go there. We can wait there until the rain stops."

Gloria and Imelda were huddled behind him as they made their way to a small overhang that barely protected them from the storm.

With every thunderclap, the two women hugged each other tighter. Kenji put his back to the rain with his arms around Imelda and Gloria to keep the rain off them. The three of them huddled together, quivering in their wet clothes quietly as the cold rain poured. Whenever the thunder exploded in its earth-shattering crashing sound right after a shocking lightning strike, the world seemed to be ending. It made them cling tighter to each other; the overhang offering them protection.

Imelda opened her eyes to see a glimmer of sunlight peeking between the swaying leaves. The rain still falling steadily but less violent. A slight wind blew the cold rain across her face. That was when she realized the storm had finally passed. She was alone with Gloria, Kenji was nowhere.

"Kenji," Imelda whispered initially. "Kenji!" she shouted when she did not get any response.

Gloria was awakened, confused. "What's going on?" she asked.

"Kenji is not here!" Imelda sounded alarmed.

Gloria's eyes opened wider in alarm. She quickly looked around, hoping to find Kenji but to no avail. "Did he leave us?" she asked.

Soon they heard the sound of machetes cutting through leaves and branches. The noise was followed by men's voices speaking in Japanese. They seem to be headed toward Gloria and Imelda's direction.

The cousins pressed closer to each other. They shuddered at the thought of being discovered by the Japanese soldiers. They prayed in earnest not to be found.

"We have to look for shelter," Itaru said to the two other soldiers.

"I agree. I'm tired. We should also look for food," said Gaku as he leaned against a tree.

"The Americans might be close behind. We should not stop," chimed in Katsuo as he pushed forward, hacking shrubs with his machete.

"Yes, but if we do not rest, we cannot fight the Americans," Itaru countered as he too propped himself against a tree.

"I am too weak and hungry. Let's set up camp here and find

food," exclaimed Gaku as he examined the surroundings.

"Ah, you two are weaklings," said Katsuo as he threw down his machete, giving up begrudgingly.

"Look!" pointed Gaku, "There is an overhang over there. We can take shelter there."

Imelda and Gloria heard them and slowly moved out of the overhang. On their hands and knees, they crawled away to a nearby clump of leaves and crouched on the ground. They were hardly breathing and strived not to make a sound.

"This is perfect," said Gaku as he started to walk towards the overhang.

"Wait," cautioned Katsuo as he put his arm up to block Gaku and Itaru from moving forward. "Someone has just been here!" he whispered softly.

"There is no one here," said Itaru looking very irritated. "Out in the pouring rain?"

"Look at the ground," pointed Katsuo as he whispered to Gaku and Itaru. Unfortunately, Imelda and Gloria left a trail on the mud when they crawled away from the overhang.

Katsuo signaled the men to be quiet as he followed the direction of the trail and it did not take long before he discovered Imelda and Gloria. He motioned to the others to surround them from the other direction.

"Ha! Got you!" exclaimed Katsuo as he grabbed both women by their hair.

The cousins cried as they were pulled up to their knees. Imelda and Gloria clung to each other, but Gaku and Itaro wrenched them apart as Katsuo inspected his find.

"Hmm… women out here in the jungle," said Katsuo as he looked at them closely. "How did you get here?"

"Who cares," said Gaku as he started to drool at the women. "I want them!" he maniacally said as he started running his hands over their breasts."

Itaro was doing the same but the women were doing their best to fight them off. Imelda and Gloria pushed the Japanese soldiers as much as they could, but the soldiers persisted and managed to pin them down. Kicking as hard as they could, the cousins were no match to the strength of the soldiers. The men had their mouths on the women's neck and chest. Imelda and Gloria cried and pleaded but it all fell on deaf ears. The soldiers started to get more aggressive and began to pull on their clothing. Katsuo ripped Imelda's shirt open, and her breast fell out.

"Nice," said Katsuo and started to fondle them.

Bang! A bullet grazed past Kastuo's cheek. Katsuo held his bloodied cheek and looked behind him in anger. It was Kenji. Realizing that Kenji was a colonel, Gaku, Katsuo, and Itaru got down on their knees and bowed to Kenji.

"So sorry, sir. We did not know that they were yours," the men said in reverence.

"Move away from them," said Kenji waving his gun at them.

The women pulled their torn clothing to cover their exposed body parts. With tears rolling down their faces, they ran behind Kenji. They were grateful to be rescued.

Kenji shot all three soldiers in the head one after the other very quickly. He did it expediently with no emotion. The cousins were shocked to see Kenji kill the soldiers!

When Imelda and Gloria got over their shock, they quickly grabbed rocks and started to pummel the soldiers with it. They were so angry and filled with fury that they did not mind blood spurting onto them as they continued to bludgeon their attackers.

Kenji had to pull them off the soldiers to stop them. As he grabbed Imelda, she turned to him with eyes ablaze with rage. He held her in his arms tightly to reassure her that she was safe now. She was stiff and lost. When she calmed a little, she began to sob loudly and as her body began to loosen up, she finally let go of the rock she was fiercely clenching.

Kenji gently rubbed her back. He pulled up her chin to look into her eyes. Tenderly, he wiped the tears from her cheeks and pulled away the strands of hair from her face. He kept nodding at her trying to reassure her that she was safe. She nodded back.

When he felt she was more collected, he looked about and paused; he was carefully considering what to do next.

"Quickly!" said Kenji, "Take off their uniforms and put them on."

Without hesitation, Imelda and Gloria quickly undressed the soldiers. Kenji disrobed and put on Katsuo's uniform.

"Why are we doing this?" asked Gloria as she was getting dressed.

"There is a big regiment of Japanese soldiers up ahead. We can join them disguised as regular soldiers. You have to cut your hair again. You must look like soldiers," explained Kenji as he took the bayonet off the rifle and handed it to Imelda for her to use on their hair.

"But surely, it will be better for all of us if you remained dressed as an officer," declared Gloria. His plan was not making any sense to her.

Kenji stopped and looked down to avoid eye contact. "Yes, but the Americans are so close behind. Should I get captured, there is no telling what they would do to me if they knew my rank," he explained.

Then he started to walk away from the women to allow them to finish dressing. After they finished cutting their hair crudely with the knife, Kenji began walking to lead the way. Both Gloria and Imelda followed him silently. The rain started to fall again as they continued their trek. The pitter-patter of raindrops was the only sound heard as all three walked for hours, single file toward the peak of Mount Malapunyo.

At one point, Kenji signaled the women to stop as he went ahead. The cousins sat down behind a shrub and waited in silence. The rain started to get heavier. A terrifying lightning strike lit the sky, followed by a deafening thunderclap. They hugged each other in fear.

They were in tight embrace when two sets of arms suddenly grabbed them from behind, holding their waist and covering their mouths. They couldn't scream and they were filled with terror again.

"Oh, no! Not again!" they both thought fearfully. Frantically, they tried to pull the hands that were holding them turned to see their captors.

When they turned around, they realized their captors were American soldiers.

Both Imelda and Gloria hugged the Americans crying and saying thank you over and over again. Overcome with joy for being rescued, they were both so relieved to be with the American soldiers.

"Sir," said the soldier to the lieutenant, "These are women, They are not Japanese soldiers."

"Great! Take them behind. The Japanese stronghold must be close. The intel is good. Let's keep going forward," the lieutenant motioned to the troops where to head out.

Before the cousins could reach the tail-end of the regiment, they heard gunshots. Everyone got on the ground. Imelda and Gloria held each other's hands while soldiers were running towards the gunfire. Only one soldier stayed with them.

Beyond the haze, Imelda caught a glimpse of Kenji near a clump of leaves to her left. She was about to move towards him but Kenji shook his head left to right. Gloria was pulling her back too.

"Hey! What are you doing? Stay down!" shouted the American soldier to Imelda.

Kenji locked eyes with Imelda and nodded. Imelda stared back. A million words were silently exchanged between them at that moment. Imelda knew Kenji was saying goodbye and she didn't want to let go, but it was time. Kenji had to escape.

Another lightning strike was quickly followed by a deafening thunderclap. When it briefly lit up the area, Imelda caught a quick glimpse of Kenji's silhouette.

"What are you looking at? Is someone there?" asked the American soldier when he noticed Imelda looking in Kenji's direction.

Kenji withdrew back into the darkness. It was the last time she saw him. Imelda knew it and she felt a sharp stab in her heart. It felt like her chest was imploding and she could not breathe. She embraced Gloria tightly and cried. "He's gone,' whispered Imelda, "Kenji is never coming back."

REJECTION OF THE HONOR BLADE

Ryan was going from one warehouse to another that was located just on the outskirts of Lipa City. There were men, women, and children milling about in tears. Each person wept for different reasons. Some cried in physical pain while others were mourning a loss of a loved one. A few were like Ryan searching for someone.

Most of them had bandages on different parts of their bodies. Some people were missing limbs, while others were lying on cots or stretchers; many were seated on the floor.

Not far away, bodies lay on the floor covered with blankets. The sight made Ryan's skin crawl. It made him feel more desperate. The urgency to find them just got more intense.

"They are alive. I will see them again. God help me find them, please," Ryan prayed nervously. He had been to several warehouses like this across the province and had not found either Imelda or Gloria.

That was when he heard her.

"Ryan, over here!" Gloria called out, waving to him with both arms.

He quickly ran towards her. Gloria practically ran into his arms. They briefly embraced until Ryan pushed back and asked, "Where is Imelda?"

"She's here somewhere," Gloria exclaimed. "Last I saw her was by the prisoner encampment."

Concern was evident on both their faces. In Ryan's mind, he could not think of any reason for Imelda to be there. Gloria had a hunch but kept it to herself.

"Let's go get her," Ryan said as he took Gloria's arm and started moving in the direction of the prisoner encampment.

Imelda was busy looking for Kenji among the captured Japanese soldiers. Her fingers clung to the chicken wire fencing as she eagerly searched for him.

Most of the captured Japanese soldiers had their heads down. The armed American soldiers had them squat in the enclosure. Several Filipinos would walk by and spit at the Japanese soldiers while shouting curse words. They were not hiding their anger against the invaders. That was why the fencing was incredibly high. Some wanted to throw rocks at the captives. They tried to hurt the Japanese soldiers just as much or even more than they were injured.

However, this did not matter to Imelda at all because she was more determined than ever to find him. She was sure of what she felt and Kenji had to know. They both had something to live for.

"Imelda!" Ryan called out as soon as he spotted her.

Gloria rushed over to embrace Imelda before Ryan got to her. "Let's go, Imelda," she said as she held her tightly. "Forget Kenji! Ryan is here now. You will be okay. Speak nothing of Kenji or anything else related to him," she cautiously whispered.

No sooner than Gloria finished her admonishment that Ryan came up to them and embraced his bride.

"I've been looking all over for you!" he exclaimed. "I promise never to leave your side again!" he said as he tearfully held Imelda tightly.

"Let's get you and Gloria all cleared, and then I will take you both back to the US on my plane. I will take you to our new home," Ryan said as he took her hand and started to lead them to an area where army jeeps were parked.

Imelda was lost in her thoughts. Her eyes were swollen from crying and her face showed no emotion. She had a dead glare. Gloria gently pushed her as Ryan held her hand.

Ryan only let go of her hand to flag down a soldier driving a jeep. He then asked the soldier if he was headed for Manila.

"Take that jeep over there," the soldier pointed to a jeep near the warehouse.

"Let's go, Imelda," Gloria said softly to her as she guided her in the direction the soldier told them to take.

Imelda looked back but Gloria nudged her and whispered, "Do not look back. There is nothing there for either of us. We need to push on and go forward for our own well-being."

Eusebia was very apprehensive as she walked through the office doors towards the receptionist's desk. The receptionist was a young lady who was busy manning the phones.

"May I put you on hold, please?" she said to the caller on the phone.

With that, she looked up at Eusebia and said, "Good afternoon. May I help you?"

Eusebia cleared her throat and answered, "I am here to see Adele. My name is Eusebia."

The receptionist instructed to sit down as she punched a button on the phone.

Adele's voice rang out from the phone's speaker, "Yes."

"Ma'am Adele, Miss Eusebia is here," the receptionist told her.

"Please send her in. Thank you," Adele replied.

The receptionist brought Eusebia to Adele's office. Adele stood up to welcome and greet Eusebia, taking her hands into her own.

"Please come in, Auntie," Adele said as she guided her to the sofa. "Have a seat."

Eusebia sat looked around Adele's office. *It's a nice and simple office,* she thought. There was a good-sized desk and a pair of chairs, a coffee table, and a sofa. One side of the room had a glass window that looked out to the plaza below. There was an orchid plant on her desk and another on the coffee table. Adjacent to the plants were pictures of Imelda, Gloria, and the twins.

"Thank you for coming, Auntie Eusebia," Adele said as she held her hands in both of hers to reassure Eusebia.

"Thank you for having me," Eusebia answered nervously.

"Would you like some tea?" Adele asked.

"Yes, please," Eusebia replied, her bag on her lap and her hands wrapped tightly around her purse.

Adele walked back to her desk and punched a button on her phone. "Tina, can you please bring us some tea and cookies? Thank you," she said.

Adele picked up a pad of paper and a pen on her desk before walking back to the sofa. She took a seat next to Eusebia and put the pad and pen on the coffee table.

"I am so glad to see you, Auntie. And thank you so much for agreeing to share your story. I understand it can be very difficult but know that it will help a lot of women," Adele said holding Eusebia's hands again.

"My being brave and sharing my story is all I have to offer for all the women. I have suffered like a dog and no one should ever be at that level," Eusebia's calmly said.

"Do you mind if I record this session, Auntie?"

"No, I don't mind Adele. Go ahead. I want everyone to know and never forget what happened during the Japanese occupation."

Tina walked in with a small teapot, cups and saucers, and a small plate of cookies. She set them on the coffee table and poured a cup of tea for Eusebia. Tina picked up a napkin and offered it to Eusebia along with the teacup.

"That will be all, Tina. Thank you," said Adele.

Adele waited until Tina had left the room before she started interviewing her aunt.

"Would you like to begin?" Adele asked as she picked up her pad and pen.

"Yes," Eusebia responded after taking a sip of tea. She carefully set the cup and saucer down on the coffee table.

Adele turned on the tape recorder and aimed the microphone towards Eusebia, who leaned over the microphone and asked, "Is this okay?"

"It's alright, Auntie, you do not have to lean over. The microphone is pretty powerful. It will be able to record your voice without any problems," Adele explained as she adjusted the microphone stand.

Eusebia smiled reluctantly and straightened herself on her seat. She took a breath and began, "My name is Eusebia. I am a Filipina and was a comfort woman during the Japanese Occupation in the 1940s."

"I was at home having just given birth a few days earlier to my son, Arnel, when the Japanese soldiers stormed my place. They kicked the doors, and one of my brothers, together with my husband, rushed to stop them from entering. In the meantime, my other brother tried to find a place for my sisters and me to hide." Eusebia started.

She took another sip of her tea before she continued, "From where I was hiding, I saw them push my brother and husband to the floor. They were shouting and asking where the women were hiding. The soldiers fanned out and found one of my sisters. They dragged her out from under the bed by her feet. She was kicking and screaming. My brother stood up, but one of the soldiers hit him on the head with the butt of his rifle."

Eusebia began to wring her hands as she continued nervously,

"My baby started to cry, and I tried so hard to hush him but he only cried louder. One of the soldiers heard him cry and followed the sound until he found us. He pulled me out by my hair, I tried to resist but I couldn't do anything because I was holding on to my baby."

Eusebia stopped for a moment. Adele reached for the recorder but Eusebia held up her hand to stop her. She took a deep breath and continued, "They dragged all of us out of the house and made us line up along the wall. One soldier took my son from me. He unwrapped his blanket and found out he was a boy. And then he threw my baby up in the air and then he sliced him with his sword as my baby fell back down."

Tears began to fall down Eusebia's face as she recounted the horrors of witnessing her own child's murder. Adele handed her a box of tissues. Eusebia took a bunch of and wiped the tears off her face.

"I went to pick up my baby, and I got hit on the back with a rifle. It caused me to fall face down on the ground. My husband ran toward me to help, but the soldier used the same sword that killed my baby to cut my husband's head off. I saw his head fly off his body and land near me. And all I could do was scream!" Eusebia was unable to control herself. Tears were now flowing like a deluge as the memories of her painful past came flashing back like she was experiencing the nightmare all over again. She was utterly inconsolable and broken.

Adele felt Eusebia's pain. She reached over to hold her hand. With her free hand, she poured a glass of water and gave it to her aunt.

Eusebia took a sip and then sat quietly, trying to regain some sense of composure. She reached for more tissue from the box and blew her nose that was now also filled with tears.

"Maybe we should stop and continue some other time," Adele

suggested, trying to comfort her.

"No, let's continue," Eusebia replied as she sat up and took a breath.

"I must have blacked out right after because I found myself on a *kariton* with other women," Eusebia continued to tell her story. "We were carted off to a red house. That was where we were housed and systematically raped day in and day out. We were beaten both in body and in spirit. There was nothing we could do."

Eusebia paused and she didn't notice that her mind went somewhere else. In her thoughts, she heard the echoes of the past, the crying, and screaming of little girls. The sparks she saw when the soldiers hit her with their fists. The salty taste of tears and blood in her mouth as she tried desperately to breathe while her nostrils were full of a mixture of mucus and blood and tears. The endless pawing and groping all over her body. The bites she suffered that tore off her flesh.

She had to close her eyes and go somewhere else to forget. To not hear. To not feel. Just go numb like jumping into an icy pool to become unfeeling where she could sink into an abyss of nothingness.

Suddenly she felt a hand on her hand. It reached for her, and it jolted her from her memories.

"Auntie Eusebia, are you okay?" Adele asked as she gently shook her hand. "Where did you go just now?"

"Nothing I want to repeat," Eusebia said with a forced smile. She pulled her sweater tighter around her. She then slowly stood up and said, "I should go now."

"I would hate for you to leave like this. You do not have to go right away. Stay awhile and have another cup of tea," Adele said as she poured more tea.

"No, thank you. I just want to go. Please," Eusebia pleaded as she was beginning to feel anxious.

"Alright. Shall I call a cab for you?" Adele asked as she gingerly held on to her aunt's arm.

"It's alright. Thank you. I can find my way home," Eusebia replied as she walked out the door.

In her rush to get out of Adele's office, Eusebia bumped into Kenji.

Without looking, she started to say, "I beg your pardon," until she looked up and saw who it was. Started, Eusebia jumped. She thought she recognized Kenji but she was not sure. She gripped her purse and continued to walk quickly away until she was out of the office and into the plaza where she stopped and took a deep breath.

In fact, she started taking many deep breaths. She was trying to control her space because it felt like everything was closing in on her. The world was spinning again and she lost her ground. She needed to center herself so she could breathe. Wanting to get away as far as possible, she started walking again, and she just kept walking.

Adele was surprised to see Kenji outside her office.

"Oh, Kenji, I was not expecting to see you here," she said. "Come in."

"I do not have an appointment. I hope it is okay that I came," Kenji told her.

"It's alright. I am just surprised," Adele said as she ushered him into her office.

"I would like to know more about what you are doing for the comfort women," Kenji said as he walked in.

"Please have a seat," Adele said as she ushered him in. "Would you like some coffee or tea?"

"Tea would be nice," he answered as he took a seat on the sofa.

"Tina, please bring us a fresh pot of tea. Thank you." Adele called out before shutting the door.

She took a seat and asked Kenji, "May I ask why the interest on comfort women? Were you placed into one of the camps in the US? I was told that when the war broke out, US citizens with Japanese ancestry were gathered and bused out to camps."

Before Kenji could answer, Tina walked in with the tea and a tea setting for Kenji. She set the coffee table and left as quietly as she walked in.

"No, I was not here at that time," he calmly said.

"I see," Adele replied as she filled his cup with tea. "I am just curious as to why you're interested."

"Like I said, I knew your grandfather Fulgencio. I see that you are very passionate about this matter and I would truly like to help with your endeavor," Kenji said with a smile.

"Well then, I am grateful for your interest and desire to help," replied Adele as she gave the cup of tea to Kenji. They both took a sip of their drink.

"As you know, there were many victims, and they are aging. They would like to die with their dignity restored. We need to advocate for them and ensure that this never happens again."

"And you believe that an apology will give it to them?" Kenji said.

Kenji noticed that Adele's face changed after he shared his apprehension.

He held up his hand and quickly said, "Ok, before you say anything, I am just playing devil's advocate. Give me your arguments and let's talk this through."

Adele relaxed and said, "Alright then. Let's begin. Ask me a question."

"Rape is a part of war. That is why there is a common phrase called rape and plunder. What makes the situation of the Filipina comfort women any different?" Kenji asked candidly.

"Yes, there is such a term as rape and plunder; however, for the Filipinas, Koreans, and Chinese, it is vastly different. This was a systematic and sustained operation. You can liken this to how the Germans committed the genocide of the Jewish people, the Imperial Japanese Army kidnapped, imprisoned, and abused these women to service their military men. The women were like parts on a production line. Sex slaves to service all Japanese military men," Adele countered. "So, this is not rape and plunder at random but extremely far from it. It was built to scale and red houses were established for this sole purpose. They were farming out these women."

Kenji nodded then argued, "In our culture, there are *geishas* and *oirans*. There is no shame about what they do. In fact, to this day, they still exist."

Adele's jaw dropped when she heard what Kenji said. "And

therein lies the problem. Women are not objects for men to use. We are not performing monkeys. And the comfort women are not *geishas* or *oirans* nor were they treated like them. They were raped, beaten, sodomized, and even killed. But the main point here is that there was never any consent! It is never okay to put your hand on any individual and force your will on them!"

Kenji paused to consider what he was going to say next.

"Plus, this is the 20th century. Women should be treated as equals! We deserve respect!" Adele said taking advantage of Kenji's silence.

"You mentioned that you want to give them back their dignity. But how?" Kenji asked.

"By uniting all the comfort women and making a statement. In fact, all women, even those who are not, should come together to support each other. This is our fight," Adele argued. "We need to be treated as equals. The comfort women have suffered worse than dogs. Any woman should not have to go through rape or any kind of abuse. We are not mere objects. We are someone's mother, daughter, sister, wife. We deserve to be heard and say our piece."

"How do you plan to execute that?" Kenji asked as he took another sip of his tea.

"Through awareness," Adele replied. "By making everyone aware, together we can make a change and ensure that this never happens to anyone again in any century. And getting an official apology from Japan is a start."

"I can tell you now that I do not think that they will get their apology," Kenji said reluctantly.

They both reflected on what he said. Adele knew it in her heart that what Kenji said was highly likely but she was not about to give up. She was adamant to keep fighting for the comfort women, for Gloria.

"Other than an apology, what else can help these women?" Kenji asked, sounding more concerned.

"Well, having more treatment centers will help. Most of them still need therapy to cope with the trauma. Others need housing. Many have lost their families in many ways – some of their family members are deceased, while others have simply been abandoned by their own families because they could not live with the shame."

Adele reached for her cup of tea and sipped before she continued.

"I would love to have a place where I could provide them with housing, where they can get in-home care for both physical and mental needs. A place where the women can live in peace free from scrutiny and constant shaming, where they can have their own community surrounded by individuals who genuinely care for their well-being," Adele explained. "I would also like to have an education center where women could be educated and made aware of their rights and options. Education and awareness will help prevent the repeat of this horrid atrocity."

"I admire your passion and tenacity," Kenji acknowledged.

He was entirely captivated by Adele. What a spirited individual; such fire! Just like her mother, Adele had dedication.

He watched every movement she made. Even Imelda's mannerisms were quite evident on Adele. She pursed her lips, just like her mother.

But there was one thing that caught his eye that was entirely unexpected. He noticed her thumb was bell-shaped. All of Adele's fingers were nice and long, but her thumb was stubbed. Kenji could not help glancing at his own bell-shaped thumb.

Kenji looked at his wristwatch and said, "I must take my leave. I have a critical appointment that I cannot miss."

"Well, this has been nice. Thank you for letting me speak my piece," Adele said with a smile as she stood up.

"No, thank you for sharing your vision with me," Kenji said as he walked himself out of Adele's office.

At the doorway, he turned around and bowed toward Adele, "You are very enlightened. I hope your vision comes to fruition soon." With that, Kenji closed the door and walked away with a huge smile on his face.

Honor What Honor

"You're here!" said Kenji with a huge smile.

"You are too," replied Imelda tentatively.

"I am so glad you came," Kenji said as he stepped towards Imelda to give her a hug.

But she took a step back. She was still unsure of what she was doing there. She quickly scanned the area to make sure no one she knew was there.

"I'm back again where we started 40 years ago. I don't even know why I am here, but I'm here," Imelda said, avoiding eye contact with Kenji.

"I'm glad that you are. I have been searching for you for an awfully long time," Kenji said. "I knew that Ryan had a plantation in Hawaii. I went there, but you were not there. Buying that plantation was my only way to you."

"Well, you wasted your time and money," Imelda retorted.

"Was I so wrong to seek you out? I came here just to see you," Kenji said as they walked to a more secluded section.

"I know it has been decades, but what I feel for you is true. I know it in my heart, so I had to see you to know if you feel the same way and if we can make a go of it," Kenji said earnestly.

"The past is the past Kenji," answered Imelda as she looked away. "There are too many hurdles, people, places, and time between us. Many will be hurt by this," she explained.

"Shouldn't we focus on the here and now? We are not getting any younger, and we do not know how much time we have left. You were hospitalized, and I had a stroke. We each have physical impairments," said Kenji as he took another step closer.

He took her hand into his and held her chin with his other hand. Kenji made her look at him as he solemnly said, "I want to be with you while you are still you, and I am still me. I want to be there to hold your hand when you start losing your sight. You can trust that I will be by your side always to care for you and love you."

Imelda tried to look away, but Kenji held her face so they could continue looking at each other. "I want to be there with you until the twinkle in your eyes dim and your mischievous smile is lost. I see you. You may not be the woman you used to be when we were younger, but I will still take all of you now as you are. In my eyes, you will never be feeble or weak. I will treasure you like the gem that you are. Holding you will be my honor, and loving you will be my privilege."

"Kenji, we both have different lives now," she replied trying to avert Kenji's eyes.

Imelda struggled to wring her hands off him and finally turned away from Kenji.

"Why now? Why can you not just go and disappear like you did then?" she asked Kenji. "You left me in my greatest need. I looked for you in the prisoner camp, and when I didn't find you, I faltered and cried many tears. I went through many years mourning you and our time together in silence. I was not even sure if you were alive. I never expected to see you again. Now here you are disrupting everything again. Why?"

Kenji put his hand on her shoulder and walked around to face her. "Seeing you again brought me so much joy. I worried and considered that you might not even want to see me. I prayed in earnest that you would grant me this wish to see you. You bring fullness to my heart."

Imelda lightly pushed Kenji away and said, "You can romanticize the past and feel all nostalgic, but don't ever forget that it was you who forced this union between us. I never asked to be in this situation. I was young and totally unaware and ill-equipped for any of it."

Kenji simply looked at her.

Imelda hesitated before she continued, "That night at the old Lucio farm and the days immediately after changed me. You put me here by your actions that evening, and for some reason, I cannot move past it."

Imelda paused and took a deep breath before continuing.

"I have had many years to think about what happened when we were young and now realize you raped me," she honestly stated. "I got you drunk, but what you did was still rape. I never gave you my consent. We never discussed it; save for your apology. And it was in your tearful apology that I forgave you."

She hesitated. Kenji was about to move closer to her, but she took a step back.

"I, too, have regrets. I will never know what it was you were going to say to me that evening. I should not have distracted you with drinking," Imelda said mournfully.

"Years later, I wondered if the tearful apology you gave while you were down on your knees was heartfelt, or just fearful of the consequences. Was I wrong to forgive you?" Imelda said as she took another step away from Kenji.

Now, with them face to face, Imelda looked at Kenji directly, confident that she could gauge the honesty of his response. "I want to know why you got down on your knees, cried, and begged for forgiveness? Was it because you cared or because you were afraid of getting in trouble for your crime?"

"Imelda..." Kenji began to say.

"It was at that moment when you were on your knees and begging for forgiveness that I felt something," Imelda interrupted him. "Why? Because if a man as powerful and important as you can apologize to someone as young and unimportant as me, then that man must have a good heart. I fell completely in love with you."

"I fell in love with you. Is it real or some form of Stockholm syndrome, I don't know? But it has tied me to you." Imelda repeated as if by repeating it, she would finally make sense of it all.

Kenji couldn't help it anymore. He quickly put his arm around her waist and pulled her to him. He held her face and kissed her. It was like how he remembered it to be — the taste of her lips, the smell of her hair, all of it.

Imelda was unable to resist Kenji. She slowly moved to embrace Kenji. His kiss felt so familiar, it took her back to the very beginning again…

Imelda woke up with a big smile on her face, and she said, "I love you, Kenji."

She felt at peace and somehow complete. She looked to her right and saw Kenji sleeping next to her with his back turned to her. She smiled and moved closer to him. Gently, she squeezed her left arm between his left arm and side to hold his chest.

Kenji felt her naked body press against him. He pushed his left leg underneath Imelda's leg. No words. Just this quiet closeness. Everything felt right with the world at that moment. Only the two of them entwined; together.

Imelda started to get up, and Kenji pulled her back. "No. Not yet. Give me just a few more minutes, please," he said.

She stopped and held on to him a little longer. Finally, she decidedly sat up. "I have to go now," Imelda said as she started to put on her dress.

Imelda pulled up to her driveway and noticed Adele's car. She got out and locked the car when she caught a glimpse of Adele looking out the window.

Adele rushed out of the house, seemingly anxious. "Mom! Where have you been? I have been looking for you for hours!"

Imelda saw the concern on Adele's face. "Why, what's the matter?" she asked.

"It's *Ninang* Gloria," Adele said. "The hospital called and said something happened and that she was asking for you. Uncle Barry, Kent, and Mary Ann are there already."

Both women quickly got into the car and drove to the hospital. As Adele drove, Imelda pulled out her rosary and started to pray. They both prayed that they were not too late.

At the hospital, they saw Kent and Mary Ann. They all hugged tearfully. Then a nurse explained that Gloria was moved to the ICU and that Barry was with her. "The patient had an episode earlier this afternoon, and it was necessary to take her to the ICU," the nurse explained.

"But she was fine this morning. I saw Gloria, and we even had a pleasant chat," cried Imelda in disbelief.

"As I stated, she had an episode, and the doctors are checking to see what they can do for her. I cannot give you details. You will have to talk to the doctor when he comes around," the nurse explained. "Only one person can enter the ICU at a time."

"Mom, you go ahead," Adele said as she gently nudged her mom towards the ICU doors.

Imelda followed the nurse to Gloria's bed. She gasped when she saw Gloria lying with her eyes closed and several lines of IVs and wires attached to her. She was wearing an oxygen mask, and Imelda could see it filled with her breath and then evaporate and then repeat again. The monitoring machines were beeping steadily.

Barry was seated next to Gloria, talking to her quietly. Whatever it was that he said, Gloria would respond with a faint smile. They were reminiscing about their past…

Gloria was coming out of the women's bathroom when she saw a pair of shoes in front of her. When she looked up, she saw Barry with a look of concern on his face.

"Are you alright?" Barry asked.

Surprised by Barry's question, she realized that she had all of her fingers in her hair, rubbing her scalp. She quickly put her hands down and answered, "Oh, I am quite alright. Thank you for asking. I was simply thinking of something."

"Nothing alarming, I hope," Barry replied as he moved closer to her.

"No, really, I am ok," Gloria answered as she took a step to leave.

Barry then reached into his pocket and gave her his business card. "I work in this building, and if you ever need anything banking related, I am your guy," he said with a smile.

Gloria smiled back and took the card. "Thank you. I just might do that," Gloria said as she started to walk away.

Days later, Barry was pleasantly surprised to take Gloria's call. She wanted to meet to discuss a banking transaction that she would need his help with.

They met at dainty coffee shop not far from where they first met. Barry got there early and eagerly waited for Gloria. He sat at a table by the window where he had a good view of the street and the entrance.

When Gloria stepped out of the taxi, the sight of her struck

Barry. She was breathtaking! He watched her walk into the restaurant. Soon enough, she walked up to their table. He was so awestruck, he couldn't form a word.

"Hi, Barry. Thank you so much for meeting me here," Gloria said extending her hand.

Barry gathered himself and shook her hand. "The pleasure is mine," he managed to say with a smile.

They both sat down and a server promptly took their order.

After the server left, Gloria got started with the business. "I asked you here, hoping you could help me set up a bank account for my group of women," she explained.

"Of course, glad to help," he said. "Tell me more about your group. Is this a business venture? What services would you need?' Barry asked.

That was when Gloria started to talk about comfort women and their banking needs. She even went further and discussed her own experience.

Barry was dumbstruck! He sat there and watched her tell her story. It was unbelievable and quite incredible. Silently, he sat there listening, captivated with Gloria and moved by her horrific story and how she wanted to make changes for other women like her. He felt her pain and anguish. He also felt her strength and determination.

During Gloria's recounting of her story, Barry wanted to be her knight in shining armor and take her away to some place safe and shield her from all her agony. But he saw that she did not need rescuing and that she was completely capable of saving herself and others. She was definitely Wonder Woman!

After their second meeting, Barry found himself in Gloria's world. He set up the bank account but did not stop there. Barry attended her fundraisers and met the other comfort women. He also met Adele and saw how they both worked tirelessly for their cause.

One evening after a meeting with the comfort women, Barry asked Gloria to have dinner with him. They went to a restaurant that overlooked the San Francisco Bay. From their vantage point, they could see airplanes landing and taking off.

After dinner, the server took away their plates and replaced it with coffee for each of them. Barry took Gloria's hand into his and said, "You are amazing! I must admit I have feelings for you."

Gloria looked at him and smiled, "I have feelings for you too."

Barry did not expect her response! He could not believe this incredible woman was also interested in him. *"Wow!"*

Gloria was a bit amused. She had an inkling of what Barry was feeling. She was initially puzzled by his actions. She thought he was just a spectator watching the circus show called the comfort women. Later on, Gloria realized that his intentions were genuine and that he truly cared about her cause. She saw the kindness in his heart through his actions; how he truly listens.

Barry, excited, kissed her like a teenager feeling his first love. When their lips parted, his eyes were filled with joy. He knew then that he had found the love of his life.

The alarm from one of the monitors attached to Gloria jolted Barry away from his reverie. A nurse came and pressed a few buttons on the machine to stop the beeping and quietly walked away.

Barry looked up and saw Imelda. He whispered something to Gloria and kissed her on the forehead. Barry stood up and hugged Imelda before he left to join Kent and Adele outside.

Imelda took Gloria's hand and squeezed it gently.

Gloria opened her eyes slowly and searched Imelda's face. When she saw her cousin, she smiled, pulled off her oxygen mask, and said, "Don't worry, I am not going anywhere without a fight."

Imelda smiled, and with another gentle squeeze on Gloria's hand, she said, "Silly, who said you are going anywhere!?"

Imelda gently put the mask back on Gloria

"Did you see Kenji?" Gloria asked as she lifted the mask again.

"Yes, I did," Imelda answered as she gently pushed the mask back down.

"Did you thank him for saving us time and again?" she asked after lifting the mask again.

"Yes, I did. Kenji said he wanted to see you, so we were planning to see you tomorrow," said Imelda.

"Ah, so you guys are together," Gloria concluded. "Took you long enough. I'm glad."

Imelda simply smiled back at Gloria.

"Imelda, I have known you my entire life. Heed what I tell you next," Gloria said in between gasps for air. "Leave Ryan. He is no good for you. He has put you in a box where you cannot grow. You were very spirited and independent, and he managed to squeeze out all the life out of you. You've changed, and it's not for the good. Living a life of quiet compliance does not suit you. You need to spread your wings. Find yourself again. With or without Kenji, you are strong. Follow your bliss."

Imelda was about to answer, but Gloria did not stop talking, "Be like Kronos. Ryan tried to control you ever since he saw you ride Kronos. And then when he got back from Hawaii, he simply took over, and you gave in."

Gloria paused and continued speaking.

"You lost your way, Imelda. You used to identify with all those heroes in your books. So full of life, willing to take on anything. You had a sense of adventure and purpose. But now, you've become a bored housewife. It's just not for you. You lost that vim you once had."

"It's probably not Ryan's fault. He doesn't know you like I do. And this…this is not you," Gloria said, waving her finger at Imelda.

Imelda nodded and said, "I know what you are saying. I was slowly feeling trapped and feeling out of place. I love Adele and will do anything for her, but I was beginning to feel that Ryan is not for me. Not because Kenji is back. This malaise was slowly growing over the years."

"Ryan is not a bad man. He is just not right for you. Remember when we were young, you said you needed a strong man, not to simply protect you but to treat you as an equal and let you grow. Ryan is not that man," said Gloria.

Despite her difficulty breathing, Gloria continued talking, confident that Imelda would finally listen to her.

"The Japanese occupation did not help things either. It changed us both. I used to follow you around in awe at everything you did. Now I feel I have to pull and push you to do anything," Gloria said. "I do not know who or what held your spirit captive. All I know is that you have changed for the worse, and I do not want this for you. Go find yourself.

Tio Fule would like you to be happy."

"Hush...stop talking, Honey. I know and trust me. I will look for her and do my best to be better," Imelda assured her as she gently squeezed her cousin's hand while holding the oxygen mask firmly on her face.

"Adele is waiting for her turn," Imelda said shortly as she kissed Gloria's forehead.

Adele was patiently waiting by the door for Imelda to come out. She quickly went in to see her *ninang*.

Imelda collapsed helplessly on the waiting room chair. She started to cry; she knew that Gloria's time was quickly running out.

CONFLICTED

Fujiko was riding Eno with gusto. Her hips were thrusting rhythmically until she achieved orgasm. She then quickly got off her lover and laid next to him, gasping for air. She pulled the blanket up as Eno reached over to cuddle.

Fujiko pushed Eno's hand away as soon as it touched her body.

"Sometimes, I feel that you are just using me for my body," Eno exclaimed as he tried to hold on to her torso.

"Don't be such a child. It's beneath you," Fujiko replied as she shifted from her back to her side, facing away from Eno.

"Hey, I can't help what I feel," Eno explained as he gave up and decidedly sat up.

Eno started to stretch and look for his pants. He found them under Fujiko's dress. While putting one pant leg on after another, he said, "I have to get to the office and finish the paperwork for the purchase of that Hawaiian plantation."

Fujiko sat up and said, "Oh, another nice gem to add to the vast portfolio of goodies!"

"Uhm, there's something different about this," said Eno as he continued to button up his shirt.

"This sale came up as a surprise," Eno said as he looked for his jacket. "Can you help me find my jacket? I have a meeting with Kenji in less than an hour about redoing his will. If I were you, I'd be careful."

"Oh please," Fujiko exclaimed. "I have him wrapped around my little finger. Don't forget, I am holding on to the ace," she continued as she kicked Eno's jacket towards him.

"Well, I am concerned," said Eno. "That plantation was never on the radar. No due diligence or comps. And when I checked, he offered them well over market price."

Fujiko sighed and exclaimed, "Oh, do not be so dramatic! You yourself mentioned just the other day that there is an unprecedented number of Japanese nationals buying up Hawaiian properties. It even made the news. The price is surely going up due to that."

Eno turned to look at her and said, "I still think there is something very personal about this sale. That Ryan and Imelda Makena must be someone important to him. I do not think it's the plantation. It does not have anything significant to warrant the price."

"Wait," exclaimed Fujiko. "Did you say Imelda?"

"Yes, Imelda and Ryan Makena. Do you know anything about them?" Eno asked as he put on his tie.

"No, but the name, Imelda. Kenji would call out her name in his sleep," Fujiko said as she put on her dress with a look of concern.

"If I didn't know better, I would say that, based on that, your boy has a thing for this Imelda," Eno said candidly.

He then checked out his reflection in the mirror to make sure his suit looked good.

"Come to think of it, he did hire a private investigator to look into their daughter, Adele. I know he got the report a few days ago. Oh well," Eno said as he dismissed its importance.

Fujiko quickly put on her dress, and, as she walked over to Eno, she said, "Zip me up."

Eno reached over to zip up Fujiko's dress, and then while looking at the mirror again, he finger-combed his hair. "I got to go," Eno said as he headed for the door.

"Wait, do you know where these people live?" asked Fujiko.

"Their information is in this folder. I will leave it here. I have to go," Eno said as he put the folder on the table and walked out.

Fujiko was sitting in her parked car for a while now. She was rubbing her hands together as she sat waiting. The fog was still heavy and visibility was abysmal. She turned on the car engine so she could put the heater on. She quickly glanced at her baby, who was sleeping in her car seat.

"This has to work," she said to herself as she tucked the blanket in around her baby gently.

She smiled at her sleeping baby and said, "You are worth all of this."

Hearing the front door close caught her attention. Fujiko quickly switched off the ignition. She looked out to see Ryan walking down the path towards his car. He got in and started the car. Ryan sat there for a few minutes before pulling out of the driveway. Fujiko slowly crouched down in her seat so Ryan would not see her as he drove past.

Once Ryan was out of view, she sat up and gently pulled her daughter out of the car seat. She opened the door and stepped out. On the sidewalk, she hesitated for a minute then proceeded to walk to the door and rang the doorbell.

It was only a couple of minutes and yet Fujiko felt it took forever for the door to open. She was so nervous as she held her sleeping baby tighter.

"May I help you?" Imelda asked when she opened the door.

"Hello, you don't know me. My name is Fujiko. This is Kenzi, my daughter with Kenji," Fujiko said, thrusting her baby girl's face at Imelda.

Fujiko's bombshell reverberated in Imelda's ears. Neither woman knew what to do next.

Finally, Imelda said, "I don't know why you're here. We have nothing to talk about." With that, she started to close the door.

"Wait," Fujiko exclaimed as she threw her shoulder to the door to stop it from closing.

"I know you are seeing Kenji! You should stop. We have a child together. My daughter and I need him to be a father to Kenzi. You can't take him away from us!" Fujiko cried out while still propped at the door.

Imelda got behind the other side of the door and pushed harder on it. She had nothing to say. What could she say? She just wanted to shut the door. She didn't want to hear anything more from Fujiko.

As the door slowly closed on her, Fujiko straightened herself and rapped on the door.

"I know you're still there! It's not right! Kenji belongs to Kenzi and me," Fujiko called out.

All the shouting caused the baby to wake up and start to cry.

"Don't take him away from us!" Fujiko yelled as she banged her fist on the door.

Fujiko shushed her baby as she walked back to her car.

Imelda was leaning on the door when tears started to run down her face. The thought that Kenji had a family never crossed her mind! The baby would hinder their plans of getting together. With a baby, Kenji has to stay with them and not her.

Being with Kenji is no longer an option. Any dreams or wishes of a life together are gone. She was stupid to think that it was easy to pick up from where they left off. Someone much younger needs Kenji more.

She looked out the window next to the door and watched Fujiko get into her car. After what seemed like forever, the engine started, and the car drove away.

Imelda's thoughts were suddenly racing. That was Kenji's family. He has a baby named Kenzi – it sounds so much like Kenji. What should she do? There is no life with Kenji now, she realized.

Fujiko was so infuriated as she got into her car. Kenzi was still crying when Fujiko put her into her car seat. She searched the baby bag for her bottle. Once Kenzi got her bottle of milk, she stopped crying.

"Kenzi will get it all. She will have it all, and I will make sure of it. I will raise her properly, and she will be famous; everything I was not," Fujiko told herself.

Then the memory of *Mamasan* made her scowl…

"This is not right!" *Mamasan* angrily shouted at Fujiko as she slammed her folded fan on the table. The teacups rattled as a consequence.

"But *Mamasan*. This is a good thing," Fujiko tried to reassure her while remaining in her kneeling seated position.

"This is not our way. What you are doing is not being *geisha*," *Mamasan* insisted, still visibly upset.

Fujiko took *Mamasan's* hand and put it on her pregnant belly and said, "With this baby, Kenji will be more than my *danna*. I can retire from this way of life."

Mamasan angrily took her hand away from Fujiko and exclaimed, "You are not doing the ways of a *geisha*. If anything, you are behaving like an *oiran*!" She forcefully stood up to end the disagreeable conversation. Fujiko was clearly errant in their ways and their tradition. She was bringing shame to her teahouse.

Fearing that she may have completely lost *Mamasan's* trust, Fujiko's started to cry. She quickly leaned forward to bow with her head on the floor towards *Mamasan* and pleaded, "But *Mamasan*, you are the only mother I know. Surely, you are happy for me and my good fortune."

"Your own mother sold you to me when you were a baby! I should have known you would bring shame to my house. Always so insecure. You were always hankering for my attention. You have disgraced this house. You are not welcome here," *Mamasan* declared as she started to walk away.

Fujiko quickly pulled on *Mamasan's* kimono and she was dragged on the floor. She cried out, "But *Mamasan*, how can you not be happy for me? Kenji has accepted this baby."

Mamasan turned around and faced Fujiko down and said, "We are artisans and not prostitutes. You have disgraced this house. Your blind ambition and scheming ways are not our ways. Nothing can be gained by deceit."

"Hello. Eno here," he said as he answered the desk phone.

"Eno, Kenji is seeing that Imelda person," Fujiko said as she held on to the receiver on the one hand and the steering wheel on the other.

"How do you know?" asked Eno as he went around his desk.

"I just came from her house. I saw her. She didn't know about Kenzi or me," explained Fujiko as she blew her horn at a passing car.

"What?!" exclaimed Eno as he sat down on his chair. "You went there? You shouldn't have!" Eno admonished Fujiko.

"Why?" asked Fujiko, surprised by his reply. "I think I have her running scared. She shut the door on me. She will go away, and that will be the end of it," she said confidently. She felt very sure that she handled the situation very well.

"I do not think so. It's more complicated than that," answered Eno as he leaned back onto his seat.

Fujiko sensed a problem. She pulled over and asked, "Why? What is happening?"

"Well, Kenji asked me to redo his will. Kenzi still has an

inheritance; I am still the executor of his estate. You are still her guardian," Eno said matter-of-factly.

"So, what's the problem? We still have control of his fortune," Fujiko questioned as she grew impatient.

"Nope. Not all of it," Eno sighed. "Kenji is leaving half to Imelda's daughter. He did not say why, but he was adamant about the change. It must have something to do with the report he got from the private investigator."

"Huh?" Fujiko exclaimed as she stared out the car window blankly, already considering her next move.

"Fujiko, are you there?" Eno called out.

"Kenji must die before he signs the new will," Fujiko declared willfully.

"It's too late. Kenji got it notarized right after he signed it," replied Eno. "And seriously, you want to murder Kenji?!"

"What?! How could you let this happen?" exclaimed Fujiko as she gripped her steering wheel.

"It was out of my hands Babe," answered Eno as he leaned forward to look at the papers on his table.

"Don't call me that, you American-born idiot! You can't do anything right!" shouted Fujiko very angrily.

"What's the matter? I let you make Kenji think Kenzi is his when surely, she is our child. Half is still a lot. We can still live very comfortably on that," Eno assured her.

"You fool! We already had the whole thing! Why should we settle for half?" Fujiko retorted. She was very agitated and she banged the receiver on the steering wheel.

Eno didn't know what to say. He was slowly losing patience. Tolerating Fujiko being with Kenji had been a bitter pill to take. Her contemptuous demeanor is definitely more than a little annoying.

"Kenji must die for this," Fujiko said with finality as she hung up.

LET IT ALL OUT

Eusebia waited patiently by the door holding a small package. Being a dreary day only dampened the gloominess. The fog came early that afternoon. It was hard to tell if it was actual rain or just heavy mist. The dew drops were beginning to pool on the hydrangea leaves growing next to the front door.

She was trying to remember when she last saw Gloria. It was a month ago at her place. Gloria's home was a small cottage behind this main house. Eusebia brought freshly made *ensaymada* from her own kitchen. Gloria was so surprised that it was still warm. They ate it with coffee under the tree just outside her cottage.

"Hello, Auntie Eusebia," greeted Adele as she opened the door.

"Good afternoon Adele," replied Eusebia.

They hugged briefly. Then Adele and Eusebia quickly wiped the tears that came consequently.

"Please come in," Adele said as she invited her in.

Eusebia walked through the door, turned around, and presented the package she was holding to Adele.

"This is baked macaroni with meat sauce. Gloria said that she and your mom liked eating this," she said as she offered the Pyrex dish to Adele.

"Oh, yum. It's one of my favorites! Thank you!" she said as she accepted the dish.

They were by the coat closet, so Adele offered to take Eusebia's coat. "May I take your coat?"

"Yes, please." Eusebia took off her coat, Adele took it and put it inside the coat closet.

"Thank you so much for coming. We will begin the novena rosary for *Ninang* Gloria in about thirty minutes," Adele said as she ushered Eusebia to the sunroom.

Adele stopped by the dining room and put the casserole dish on the dining table next to other dishes. There were quite a number of dishes surrounding a vase filled with pink gladiolas, which were Gloria's favorite flowers. The floral arrangement towered over a variety of dishes; a testament of how Gloria rose above other comfort women and looked after them.

The sunroom was actually a greenhouse attached to the main house. It was adjacent to the den that was next to the dining room. The three sides of the room and roof were made of glass. Plants were all around. One wall had orchids hanging off the branches of a large piece of driftwood. Some of the plants were in pots on the floor, while others were hanging from the ceiling. It was beautiful and warm in that room, like the Garden of Eden, perhaps. It felt warm and healing.

In the sunroom, there was a small statue of the Virgin Mary, a crucifix, and a portrait of Gloria. There were more gladiolas on the same table. A pair of candles with a basket full of rosaries were also on the table. It was neatly placed next to glass panels that looked out to the garden where one could catch a glimpse of Gloria's cottage.

It started to rain. Everyone could hear the pitter-patter of rain on the plated glass. It started slow, then became a steady downpour. Light slowly flooded the room. All the glass reflected the glow from the warm globe mercury lights. It bounced all over, making the room very warm, very comforting. For a sad day, it felt like they were basking in a loving, blessed moment of light.

Imelda, Adele, and Kent were milling about. Many of the women made their way to Imelda and Kent to offer their condolences. They told both Imelda and Kent how much Gloria meant to them and how her passing was a loss for all of them.

Barry was there. He was terribly heartbroken and he sat in the corner all alone. Everyone noticed that he was overcome with grief, so they opted to leave him alone. Those who knew him well politely approached him, said a few words as they touched his shoulder.

Ryan walked up to Barry and whispered something to him. Barry nodded as he looked blankly at him. Ryan then pulled up a chair and sat quietly next to him.

Margaux tugged on Kent's hand. "Can we go see *Lola* Gloria now?" she asked innocently.

Kent squatted down to face her squarely and said, "Honey, *Lola* Gloria went to heaven."

"When is she coming back?" Margaux pressed on.

Kent started tearing up. He didn't know how to explain it to her.

Mary Ann walked up to them. She was carrying Johann, who was sound asleep. She slowly crouched down and held Kent's hand.

"Margaux, *Lola* Gloria is gone, and she will not be coming back," Mary Ann tried to explain.

"But I want *Lola* Gloria!" Margaux insisted as she started crying.

Adele joined them and took Margaux's hand and said, "Hey Margaux. *Lola* Gloria is getting heaven ready for all of us. We will meet her there."

"Let's all go to heaven now. I want to see *Lola* Gloria!" Margaux said as she stomped her feet defiantly.

"Oh honey, I want to see her, too," Adele said as she embraced Margaux, who was now beginning to cry inconsolably.

Mary Ann took Margaux's hand and tugged at her gently, telling her, "Let's go upstairs and put Johann to bed. Then we can continue reading Charlotte's Web. You like that, yes?"

Margaux nodded and rubbed off the tears on her face. Kent took Johann from Mary Ann and started walking up the stairs. Mary Ann and Margaux were still holding hands as they followed Kent upstairs.

Later on, Imelda lit the candles while Adele handed out rosaries to those who did not bring one. They began to pray the rosary solemnly. They sang Fatima songs accompanied by someone playing the guitar. When they finished, the women took the time to talk about how Gloria helped them. There was such an outpouring of love that there was not a dry eye in the room.

Imelda looked around the room. *"They all love her,"* she thought to herself. She felt a warmth developing from deep within her. This circle of family and friends was an intimate group who genuinely cared for each other. Imelda avoided this group because she did not want to be identified as one of them: *"the comfort women."*

Imelda was surprised about how much they genuinely cared for Gloria. Their shared history drew them together, and their advocacy sustained them. They were not crying out about being victims but about what they have done in spite of it. They were not the blight but the answer.

Barry stood up and went to the center of the room. Everyone fell silent and waited for him to speak.

Barry swept his gaze across the room. He looked sullen and was trying to suppress himself from crying. "Thank you, everyone, for coming. I am sure Gloria is happy to see all of you here…" He struggled to talk and took a moment before continuing his address.

"For those who do not know me, I am Barry, Gloria's husband. She was the love of my life. I never thought I would find love, but I found it with Gloria. I usually call her my crazy wife. If you know her, you would know that she is quite mischievous." He stopped after his last statement stirred a faint laughter in the room.

"Yes, she would always find something witty to say, especially at moments like this," Barry continued as tears began to well up in his eyes.

"You know, we almost didn't get together. Gloria was apprehensive, and rightfully so, after two marriages. Who could blame her? But then again, she was always hopeful," Barry related, which drew nods of agreement from a few people in the room.

"Before we got married, after a very trying day, she wanted to break it off with me. She told me, 'I love you, but...' I stopped her before she could continue, I told her that our love does not have 'buts.' That no matter what her past was, we are building our future together. That we will own our destiny together and we will not allow it to own us."

He took a brief pause and smiled a little bit at the thought of him and Gloria together.

"Gloria's wish was for this movement to continue even without her. To garner the respect and dignity that all of you deserve. Gloria may be gone, but her spirit lives in this movement. Let us keep her legacy alive."

Barry bowed his head after he ended his address and wiped away his tears. He slowly walked out of the room. Kent met him at the door and hugged him.

After Barry, a young lady took to the the center of the room. She introduced herself as Remy and said that she wanted to say something about Gloria. Everyone fell silent and turned their attention to her.

Remy began by saying, "I met Auntie Gloria a few years ago. What struck me about her was how independent and outspoken she was. She was very open about her story. She knew the consequences and lived with it unapologetically.

"Auntie Gloria reinvented herself. She fought the "damaged goods" or "a big mistake" label. Wallowing in pity was something she had strong feelings against. She was driven to move on. She would say, "Oh, boohoo. You are still here, so you can still do something about it."

A chuckle came from the group as they recognized Gloria's commonly used expression.

"She told her story about being a comfort woman, how she was a victim at the hands of the Japanese army. About what she had to do to stay alive. But that was not all she talked about," Remy continued. "She talked about redemption. She said, to sit and do nothing was not acceptable. To do so meant that they won. It was admitting defeat."

Everyone nodded in agreement.

"She said that this should not be taboo. That the power to change is within us, and that banding together gives us more power. Individually we are just a trickle, but together, we can be a flood. A force to be reckoned with."

Remy paused briefly, scanned the room and locked eyes with Adele before she continued.

"Although I was born after the war, this is also my fight. Like Auntie Gloria said, this is bigger than any of us. And not isolated to the events in the 1940s. It's about respect and dignity. And that sexual abuse should stop.

"I will fight for my mother, my sister, and my future daughters and nieces. I will continue Auntie Gloria's legacy. I will advocate for justice and change.

"Thank you, Auntie Gloria, for opening my eyes and leading the way. We will keep up the fight for justice and affect change for the future of all women," Remy said and finally concluded her speech.

The crowd clapped their hands and nodded. Yes, this was what Gloria wanted. They all agreed that it was necessary to push on.

The doorbell rang. Adele walked to the front door to answer it. When she opened the door, she found Kenji standing outside holding an umbrella.

"Come in. So glad you could make it," Adele said as she pulled the umbrella basket towards Kenji.

Kenji closed the umbrella and shook off the water from it before he entered the house and placed the umbrella in the basket.

"I hope I am not too late," he said apologetically to Adele. He looked around the room while taking off his coat. "I found out about this not too long ago."

"It is alright. What is important is that you are here," Adele reassured him as she took his coat from him and put it in the coat closet.

They proceeded to walk to the sunroom. Kenji was eager to see Imelda. He knew how close she was to Gloria. Although they were cousins, they grew up practically as sisters. He had to control himself so he would not try to reach out to her so publicly.

He stood by the French doors to the sunroom, scanning the room, searching for Imelda.

In the other end of the room, Eusebia was looking for Adele. She wanted to leave early but she wanted to talk to Adele first. Eusebia saw Adele standing near the French doors. She walked towards Adele. When she was came close, she saw the same, familiar face standing behind Adele again. And it struck her, finally. Eusebia recognized Kenji! He was with that monster, Akito!

Eusebia felt her legs go limp and she started screaming! Everyone was startled and turned around to look at her to find out what was going on. Her body was shaking as she slowly lifted her hand and pointed at Kenji and shouted, "He was one of them! Those Japanese pigs!"

Imelda, who was on the other side of the room, gasped and tried to get to Kenji right away.

Adele was surprised by this revelation and stood there looking at Kenji, unable to say anything.

Kenji, embarrassed, looked around the room and saw the angry faces staring back at him. He quickly turned his back and started to head to the front door. He stopped by the coat closet to grab his coat. He opened the front door before he could even put his jacket on. He hurriedly walked to his car without noticing that he was already getting wet.

When he reached his car, he was surprised to find Fujiko standing next to it.

"What are you doing here?" Kenji exclaimed as he walked towards her.

"You had to come to see her, didn't you," she shouted back at him.

She was standing there in the pouring rain without an umbrella, wearing just a trench coat. Fujiko was already drenched. Her long black wet hair clung to her face, neck, and shoulders. This time the rain was torrential. It rained so hard that visibility became extremely poor.

"Huh, what?!" Kenji replied, looking confused.

"You had to come and see Imelda. After everything I have done for you! After all those years. I believed I could stop being a *geisha*. But I was not enough for you." Fujiko shouted at Kenji. She was crying but her tears were being washed from her face by the rain. She was furious and hurt at the same time.

"Fujiko, get in the car! We can talk about this later," he ordered her as he opened the car door.

Imelda grabbed an umbrella before stepping out in the rain.

Quickly, she ran out, trying to catch up with Kenji. Imelda did not see Fujiko because the umbrella obstructed her view.

"Kenji!" she exclaimed when she reached him.

Kenji turned around to find Imelda standing close to him. They briefly smiled at each other, but Fujiko shouted at them, "Hey!"

"Go back to the house, Imelda. I will call you later," he said as he gently pushed her to turn back.

Fujiko was consumed by rage when she saw his concern for Imelda.

"No!" she screamed at them. "It all ends here now!" She pulled out a gun from her pocket and pointed it at Imelda.

Kenji saw the gun and realized that Fujiko was going to shoot Imelda.

Before Fujiko could pull the trigger, Kenji stepped in front of Imelda and took the bullet that was meant for her.

Imelda caught Kenji as he fell back into her arms. With his back on her chest and her arms under his armpits, she slowly kneeled so she can help him sit on the pavement. With her arms still wrapped around him, her hands found the gunshot wound, and she pressed firmly on it.

Realizing what she did, Fujiko quickly put the gun in her pocket, took the car keys from Kenji, got in the car, and hastily drove away.

"Hold on, Kenji. Hold on!" Imelda was screaming and crying at the same time.

"Imelda, I have something for you," Kenji said softly as he reached for his pocket.

"Shush, don't speak. Just hold on, Kenji," Imelda said in between sobs, still pressing on his wound. His warm blood was pooling around her fingers. It mixed with the cold rain and soaked his shirt.

Kenji strained to pull out the small box from his pocket with his left hand. He slowly lifted his hand and reached for her left arm. He placed the precious box in her hand and kept his hand on hers.

"I have been waiting to give this to you for a very long time," he said with a faint smile. Blood was slowly coming out of his mouth.

"Hush Kenji. I just want you to hold on. You can give it to me later," Imelda cried as she kissed his face with tears continuing to fall down her face.

But Kenji pressed the box into her hand harder and declared his undying affection for her. "Take it, please. I love you, Imelda. I always loved you." His eyelids fluttered, and his breathing became labored. Then it happened. His left hand fell off Imelda's hand.

Imelda embraced Kenji tighter and wailed, "No, Kenji! Please hold on! Kenji!"

The sound of sirens was getting louder as they got closer. Then the flashing lights seemed to be bouncing around as a police car, a fire truck and an ambulance pulled in. The firemen walked the perimeter to secure the surroundings. A pair of police officers got out of their car and began giving orders to the crowd gathering around Imelda and Kenji. They also cleared a path for the paramedics who pulled out a stretcher from the ambulance. They rushed to Kenji to administer to his needs.

"We will take care of him, ma'am," one of the paramedics told Imelda as he pulled her away from Kenji.

They proceeded to work on Kenji after putting him on the gurney. Sequentially, they quickly took him into the ambulance. Imelda promptly climbed into the ambulance as well and held on to Kenji's hand. The paramedic closed the door of the ambulance and drove away with the sirens blasting.

Hours later, Imelda's self-control was just about gone when she reached her garden. As she knelt by her flower bed, she felt her strength slowly and surely flowing out of her. If she could only melt into the ground, she would have. She felt like she was falling into a bottomless pit. There was nothing there. Simply nothing. She was alone, and the pain was like a darkness enveloping her with constricting silence and emptiness.

Her ride home from the emergency room was quiet and uneventful. She plainly walked out of the hospital, hailed a taxi, and sat quietly for the duration of the trip. When she got home, she went straight to her garden where she let go of all her emotions.

Brightness broke Imelda's downward spiral. Ryan turned on the lights in the garden. He slowly walked towards Imelda.

Imelda started pulling at the flower bed. The ground was still wet from the late afternoon rain. Soon Imelda's hands were muddy.

"Honey," Ryan called out. "Let's go inside," he coaxed her as he put his hand on her shoulder.

Imelda pulled away. "I have to pull out the weeds," she said. "I cannot have them take over my flower bed."

Ryan got down on one knee and embraced his wife. He held her tight and said, "Honey, it's okay. You can do that tomorrow morning."

"I can't," Imelda exclaimed. "They will take over the whole garden!" She resumed pulling anything and everything furiously. Her hand got caught on a thorn and began to bleed.

Ryan saw her hand bleeding. He grabbed both her hands and shouted, "Stop!"

Imelda stiffened up. She looked at her hands and then at the clump of leaves and flowers by her knees.

With one hand, Ryan held her chin and pulled Imelda's face to look up into his eyes. A thousand words were exchanged by merely looking into each other's eyes. An unspoken conversation was taking place. The pain, frustration, and helplessness were met with patience, understanding, and love.

Soon, they found themselves in each other's arms. Tightly, Ryan and Imelda held each other. Imelda began to cry. It started as a gentle sobbing. Soon, she was seriously wailing as her tears came down in torrents. Time stood still as they held each other kneeling on the ground.

After what felt like an eternity, Ryan got up and pulled Imelda to her feet. He held her hand and gently ushered her to the nearby bench. They sat there with her hand in his.

Ryan pulled a handkerchief from his pocket with his free hand and gave it to Imelda. She took it from him and proceeded to dry her tears.

"You know that it is all right to say it," Ryan calmly said.

Imelda stiffened again and was about to pull her hand away, but Ryan just held on to it firmly.

She looked at him questioningly.

"I know," Ryan said gently.

Their eyes met. Imelda quickly understood what Ryan was trying to tell her. "How did you know, and when did you know?" she asked in quiet disbelief.

"I've known for a very long time, Honey," he said plainly.

"What is it that you know?' she asked him patiently, wanting to be sure that they were referring to the same thing.

"About how you suffered like Gloria," Ryan answered calmly.

Imelda pulled away and said, "You knew all this time that I was one of those comfort women, and you did not say anything?"

As she spat out those words, a maelstrom suddenly formed. The heaviness lifted. The years of silence that held her gagged and bounded were ripped-off! It was replaced with sheer unadulterated hate and anger and it consumed her. Imelda imploded and exploded at the same time. She lost herself and everything happened so quickly. Only afterwards did Imelda feel the sting on her palm from slapping Ryan.

He caught her hand before she could swing it again. "I guess I deserve that," Ryan quietly declared.

"How?" Imelda asked as her tears started to fall again.

"You had nightmares. You were kicking, crying, and screaming. You even called Kenji's name while you slept," Ryan explained.

"I should have said something, done something, anything," Ryan continued as he looked away, far away, trying to find the words to console Imelda.

"Why didn't you?" Imelda asked, confused.

"I was waiting for you," he said as he held her hand tightly. "I committed myself to do whatever you decide to do."

Imelda stared at her husband with disbelief.

"What a coward, I know," Ryan said as he looked down. "At first, I was afraid to say anything. I was ashamed and feared being ostracized. You saw what happened to Gloria and her family."

Gloria stayed silent, staring questioningly at Ryan.

"I know it was my fault. I should not have left you there. I should have taken you to Hawaii with me. I could have ensured your safety," he continued to explain.

Ryan glanced at Imelda, looking for a sign as she continued to stare at him blankly.

"Honey, I wanted to defend your honor more than anything. I could have ripped-off the heads of every Japanese soldier for you. I wanted to do so much. If you had just said something," he explained.

He was at a loss. He wasn't sure if he was saying the right words to console and convince his wife.

"But you said nothing. Not a word. I have been waiting for you to say something. I wanted to respect your wishes. I was duty-bound to follow your lead. You kept silent, and that silence bounded my hands," Ryan explained.

"Your private hell became my dungeon. It was my punishment for not being there for you," Ryan said as he pulled her hand to his lips.

"I shared your pain in silence. It pained me to see that the Imelda I left behind was seriously wounded. I held onto you every night, but you were so much like a child that was so hurt. You cried in my arms all those nights. It was not easy, especially when Kenji showed up," Ryan said.

"In my mind, I had imagined a million different ways to make him suffer for all the pain he inflicted on you. I was praying that you would just say the word and I would pounce on him.

"And yet, you didn't. I was confused. Then I realized that there was something between you and Kenji. Was there?" Ryan asked while trying to look into her eyes to find the answer.

"He said he loved me," Imelda whispered but kept her head bowed, hiding her face as if it would betray what she truly felt.

Ryan shut his eyes tightly, suddenly feeling a pang of jealousy. "This cannot be," he said, as tears slowly formed on his right eye.

"Did you care for him?" Ryan asked as he gripped her hand tighter.

"Ryan, Kenji was no saint," Imelda explained. "But he did take care of Gloria and me. He did not have to, but he did. He rescued us many times over during the occupation. He was not always successful at stopping the soldiers from attacking Gloria and me, but Kenji and I had a past before the Japanese occupation. He guaranteed our safety."

"You're saying this happened before we were married?" Ryan asked in surprise. "You were with him?"

Imelda glared at Ryan.

"What?!" she exclaimed. "How dare you ask!"

"I am a man, Imelda." Ryan quickly replied. "I needed to know. I didn't really want to hear it, but I needed to know."

"Do you know how selfish and stupid you sound right now?" Imelda asked incredulously.

"I sort of knew. It is just different hearing it directly from you."

"Ryan, you pushed me to get married to you. You did not give me a choice when you asked Papa to marry me in front of the whole town!" she reminded him.

"Oh God, Imelda," Ryan said as he embraced her. "I wish I could take all of this away if I could only erase the past. You are mine, and no one else!"

Imelda pushed him away. "Are you sure? The Imelda you knew is not here. She died from a million bayonets decades ago," Imelda stated.

"Honey, I stood by your side all these years. I'm not about to leave you now. You deserve a wonderful and loving life. I will do everything to give you that life. I am here for you. I love you, and that will never change." Ryan said, hoping to comfort Imelda.

"How do I know?" Imelda asked. "I could wake up one morning to find you gone. I can't stop you, and I won't. If you stay, I want it to be because you want to. That you can honestly look at me and know that you accept me for what I am – all the filth and stigma that I carry."

Ryan put his fingers on Imelda's lips to stop her from talking. With tears in his eyes, he looked into Imelda's eyes. "No, I don't see any of that."

He held both of Imelda's hands and gently kissed each one and said, "I am sorry for all the pain I caused you. I will never ever leave you again."

"Imelda, there is no one else in this world that I love more than you. You are my princess from the first time I ever saw you. You have held the keys to my heart all this time. I can never see you as anything else but my Imelda.

"What you call filth, I see nothing but badges of honor. Stigma? All I see is fortitude. Anyone less would have surrendered and succumbed to the monstrosity that the evils of war brought.

"Instead, my Imelda held strong and kept the people she loved safe. I'm sure your Papa is proud of you. Gloria is grateful." Ryan elucidated.

"But what about you?" asked Imelda as she stared at him. "What is in it for you?"

"My princess, I thank God every day that I am with you. I cannot live without you. I am nothing without you. My heart, my love, you have suffered in silence for far too long." Ryan said woefully.

"It is true that I remained silent for fear of being ostracized. But I also did it for you." Imelda said. "I did not want to bring you shame."

"Honey, you should not have thought that way," Ryan said. "You should have said something sooner. It was my fault that you went through that awful hell."

He embraced Imelda.

"I have been here for you all this time. I will never leave you. I need you more than you think. I promise you that I will stand by you forever. I love you." Ryan said softly to her.

Imelda pulled back and trained her eyes on Ryan. And she knew. Through their shared tears, she knew that he was telling the truth.

"I wish we had talked about this sooner," Imelda cried, believing that it was all too late now.

"It does not matter. We have now, and we can move forward," answered Ryan as he so desperately tried to convince Imelda.

"But what you do not know is that Kenji and I were in love. We had been even before the occupation. Our lives just took us down different paths." Imelda explained.

"It took you to me. You are mine now," Ryan claimed while putting his hand on hers.

"I do not belong to anyone," Imelda answered as she gently pushed him away.

"This quiet denial we have kept all these years has taken a toll on us," she explained. "The silence made us grow apart. We have both changed. And I do not like who I have become."

Ryan looked down and said, "Where do we go from here?"

Imelda looked away and said, "I don't know..." She paused before turning to face him and said, "We are definitely not the same people from before the war."

"I told you that I do not care about what happened to you during the occupation," he said exasperatedly.

"That was it! You did not care, and now so much has happened since. I am not the same, and I am not sure I like who I am now either," Imelda explained.

She took a breath and continued, "I have to make changes. I want to get back on the path I was on before the war. I may not be the same person who started down that path, but I still want to accomplish some of those dreams and goals for myself. True, I may not be the same person, but I would like to think that I am better equipped now to fulfill those goals."

With every minute that she and Ryan have been talking, Imelda grew more confident and determined. She looked at Ryan and said, "I want to find my spirit and energy and push on. I want to see the world, learn, do things, be me."

Ryan took her hand again and said, "We can still do that

together."

Imelda pulled her hand away and said, "That is the thing. I feel I have to make this journey by myself. I have to find myself again. See what I have lost and know if I still want it. Unless I do all that and be kind to myself, I cannot begin to live or be able to give. My spirit died a long time ago."

Ryan started to say something but Imelda held up her right hand to stop him. She said, "It was not your fault. I just stopped living. I put myself in a box and sealed it shut. But now I want to come out and live."

"Where does that put us?" Ryan asked Imelda, imploring.

Imelda put her hand on his lap and said, "I cannot ask you to wait. I do not know how long it will take me. You should start doing your own thing."

Ryan placed his hand on top of Imelda's and said, "I will wait for you no matter how long it will take."

"Please don't. You deserve a life. We all do," she said, her voice firm and determined.

Ryan sighed and hung his head low. He was gradually realizing the extent of all the revelations. The truth had reared its ugly head. There were no more secrets. Everything was out in the open. And yet, in the here and now, he found himself left behind. All is in the past.

IT'S ALL ABOUT CLOSURE

Adele rushed to embrace Imelda. "Mom, I am so glad to see you and that you're safe!" she exclaimed. She did not expect to find Imelda in her office when she opened the door.

Imelda was caught by surprise by this. She stood up and hugged her daughter back, but the concern was still evident on their faces. Imelda was dreading this visit. That was why she waited almost a week before seeing Adele.

"I hope you do not mind. I asked Tina to let me in," Imelda explained.

"Of course not! I am just glad that you're here. Come, sit," Adele said as motioned Imelda to sit at her cozy seating area next to the glass window.

There was a shower of rain that lightly danced on the spring flowers. A few rain droplets stuck on the glass. Spring was beckoning, welcoming the start of new beginnings.

Adele asked, "Would you like coffee and doughnuts or Madeleines, Ma? I can have Tina get us some. I will be having coffee myself."

"Sure, I will take a regular coffee," Imelda answered.

Adele proceeded to walk behind her desk and opened her drawer to put her purse inside. She then pressed the intercom button.

"Tina, please bring us coffee and Madeleines or doughnuts. Thank you," she said.

She then took a seat next to Imelda and said, "I came by the house several times, but Pops said that you were not there and that he did not know where you were. What is going on?"

"We have a lot to talk about," said Imelda. "Maybe you would like to wait for your coffee. I asked Tina to clear your schedule for the next few hours. I hope you do not mind."

There was a soft knock. Tina opened the door and brought in the coffee pot and Madeleines. She set them on the coffee table and quietly walked out of the room.

"I cannot believe you got shot at! Who was that woman, Fujiko? Why would she want to kill you? Why would Kenji take a bullet for you? What is going on? Are you okay? Where have you been?" Adele asked in quick succession.

Imelda put her hand on Adele's and said, "I am alright, Adele. I had to leave the house because there were so many reporters asking a lot of questions. I had to get away."

"But you did not tell anyone where you were. I was so worried!" Adele said emphatically. That is when her eyes started to brim with tears.

IMELDA
Transformed

"Oh, honey," said Imelda as she embraced Adele. "I am ok. Everything will be alright," she reassured Adele.

"So, who is Kenji? And what is he to you?" asked Adele, still holding Imelda's hand.

Imelda took a deep breath before answering, "Kenji is…"

The intercom went off and interrupted Imelda.

"Wait a minute," Adele said while wiping her tears. She stood up and walked to her desk. She quickly pressed the intercom button and said, "Tina, were you not instructed to hold all calls and clear my calendar for today? I cannot be disturbed, please."

"There is a lawyer here," Tina informed her over the intercom. "His name is Eno Ituro. He does not have an appointment, but he is quite insistent on seeing you. He said he represents the estate of Kenji Kobayashi. He has something important to give you."

Adele looked at Imelda. Imelda nodded at Adele to indicate she should let him.

Adele hesitated before pressing the button to say, "Let him in."

The door opened, and Eno walked inside. He was carrying a briefcase, but extended a hand to Adele and said, "Thank you for seeing me. I am Eno Ituro, and I represent the estate of the late Kenji Kobayashi."

Adele shook his hand. "This is my mother, Imelda Makena. I hope you do not mind that she remains present," she said, pointing to Imelda.

Eno bowed towards Imelda and walked in the direction of Adele. "May I?" he asked while gesturing to Adele to see if he could put his briefcase on her desk.

"Go ahead," she replied.

Eno put down his briefcase and opened it. He pulled out a leather-bound binder and a large envelope and handed them to Adele.

He then said, "As the late Kenji Kobayashi's executor, I am fulfilling the instructions as written in his last will and testament. These belong to you."

Surprised, Adele accepted the leather-bound binder and the envelop. "Thank you, but are you sure this is for me?" she asked.

"I am quite certain," Eno replied. "Mr. Kenji Kobayashi made you his sole beneficiary. He executed his will on the morning prior to his untimely death."

Imelda and Adele were surprised by what Eno told them.

Eno could not tell them that this was what set Fujiko off...

"You what?!" Fujiko shouted at Eno that morning.

"I had to tell him," Eno answered as he was putting papers into his briefcase.

"You told Kenji that we are in a relationship?" Fujiko asked, clearly annoyed.

"Look, we do not need Kenji or his money. We can raise our own daughter by ourselves. I make enough money," Eno explained as he turned to face her.

Fujiko sighed and said, "It is that stupid pride of yours."

Eno pulled out a small box and dropped to his knee and said, "Marry me, Fujiko."

"Are you nuts? Why the hell would I do that?" Fujiko exclaimed as she pushed away the box.

"Because it is honorable. You no longer need Kenji as your *danna*. I can take care of you and our daughter," Eno explained.

"You are stupid. You ruined everything! I have worked so hard. Why would you ruin that?" Fujiko retorted, clearly infuriated.

"I told him that I wanted you to retire and marry me," Eno said calmly.

"You know that I am a *geisha* and not an *oiran*. You, being a third-generation American Japanese do not understand the very distinct difference between the two," she exclaimed exasperatedly.

"So, what? Marry me. Leave this way of life. I have enough money. I can maintain your lifestyle. We can live here in San Francisco and leave your past behind," Eno pleaded.

"Oh, my God! You do not get it! I do not want you. Never did! Never will," Fujiko exclaimed.

Eno stiffened as he stood up. He opened his briefcase, threw the box holding the ring inside, and locked the briefcase closed.

"I have had it with you! You are abusive and clearly not good enough to raise our daughter!" he shouted back.

"Good luck with that," she answered back. "You cannot do any better raising Kenzi much less showing her our culture!"

"You have a thwarted idea of *geisha*! You are no more *geisha* than I am Japanese!" Eno exclaimed.

"What do you know about our culture for you to say that?" retorted Fujiko.

"I know well enough to know that you have trashed the whole *geisha* concept to suit your needs while completely disrespecting all its traditions and customs!" Eno snapped back.

"You never grew up in Japan and had no idea of what you are talking about! You idiot!" Fujiko yelled back.

"Well, I told Kenji that Kenzi is my daughter and not his. And seriously, naming her Kenzi for Kenji is nuts! If anything, you are trying too hard," Eno exclaimed.

"You told Kenji that our baby is not his? Why did you tell him that?" Fujiko screamed.

Eno picked up his briefcase and said, "Because it is the honorable thing to do."

"You and your stupid honor! I was aiming for something bigger," she shouted back.

"Well, say goodbye to that. Kenji signed his new will this morning, and he is leaving everything to Adele Makena. He is on his way now to Imelda Makena's house to tell them," he said as he walked out the door and slammed it shut.

Now Eno wished he had not said any of that to Fujiko. If he did not, Fujiko would not be in jail and Kenji would still be alive.

"I do not understand. Why?" Adele asked, jerking Eno out of his deep thought.

"There is a letter there for you and your mother. I believe it will explain everything," Eno said.

He pointed to the envelope that Adele was holding.

"I will take my leave now. Should you have any questions, here is my business card," Eno said as he gave it to Adele. He turned to bow to Imelda and followed Adele to the door.

"Thank you, Mr. Ituro," Adele said as she opened the door and let him out.

"You're welcome," Eno bowed before heading out.

Adele rejoined her mother and took a seat next to Imelda. She put the binder on the coffee table. Adele held the envelope tentatively, giving her mom another look. She and her mother spent nearly a minute looking at each other.

"I think you should open it and find out what he has to say," Imelda eventually said.

Adele took a breath before she opened the envelope. True enough, there were two smaller envelopes inside. One was addressed to Imelda and the other to her.

Adele opened the envelope addressed to her. Inside, she found a letter. She unfolded the letter and started to read it.

To Imelda, it seemed that it took Adele forever to read the letter. By looking at the changing expression on Adele's face, she could see that Adele was extremely shocked by what it contained. Finally, Adele put down the letter and looked at Imelda in complete bewilderment.

"Well, what does it say?" Imelda curiously asked.

"He gave me everything!" Adele said, dumbfounded.

"What?" Imelda exclaimed.

Adele gave the letter to Imelda. "Take a look," she said.

Imelda took the letter and started reading it.

"Kenji also gave me the Hawaii plantation he bought from Pops so that I can use it for my foundation for the comfort women! He also designated a large amount to fund this foundation. I can now afford to house these women and provide both medical and mental health care for them. I cannot believe it!" Adele said ecstatically.

Imelda finished reading the letter and put it down. She could not find the words to say to her daughter.

Adele took the envelope for Imelda and pressed it into her hand. "Please read it, mom," she said.

Imelda opened it and found a folder and a letter. On the folder, Adele Makena was written on it. Inside was Adele's photo, her birth certificate, and a report from a private investigator. Imelda unfolded the letter and began reading it. Soon enough, tears started to roll down her face. She put down the letter and fold it up.

"Mom, what did he say," Adele asked.

"He figured it out," Imelda said in a soft voice as she gave Adele the folder and all its contents.

"Huh," Adele remarked, looking very confused as she reviewed all the documents.

"Kenji figured it out. He knew that you are his daughter," Imelda said delicately.

"What?!" Adele exclaimed in disbelief.

"Kenji is your biological father," Imelda revealed. She looked at Adele and gave her a moment to let it sink in.

"Explain how I am his daughter," Adele said, sounding very confused.

"I have a secret. In fact, I have many secrets, and it is time that you know the whole story," Imelda explained.

Adele could only stare back at Imelda. She was utterly overwhelmed. "*What is she talking about?*" Adele was thinking. It was just too much information being thrown out there so quickly.

Imelda stood up and walked toward the glass window. Imelda looked out while considering how she would tell Adele everything. Taking a deep breath, Imelda mulled over her dilemma. She dreaded this moment but there was no turning back now.

Imelda took a deep breath again before she began. She recounted all the events starting from the very beginning, the day she got Kronos.

When she was done, Imelda turned around to face Adele and said, "I was a comfort woman together with your *Ninang* Gloria. We were captured, and Kenji was a colonel and saved us. He took us away from all that. Kenji and I continued our relationship until the liberation. You are a product of that union."

Adele remained quiet all throughout. She was overwhelmed by the flood of information coming from her mom including what happened during and after Gloria's celebration of life. She revealed all her secrets and spared nothing.

"This is madness, mom. How can you be sure about Kenji being my father?" Adele finally asked.

"You both have a clubbed thumb. It is a genetic trait. Kenji's thumb is clubbed, too," Imelda answered.

Adele took a look at her hands, more importantly at her thumb. And that is when it finally sunk in.

"But what about Dad? Does he know?" Adele asked.

Imelda looked away and said, "Yes, your dad knows now."

Adele leaned back and exclaimed, "Oh my god, I am the daughter of a rapist!"

With her voice quivering, Adele continued, "My father was one of those who abused the very comfort women I am fighting for!"

"No, Adele! You have it wrong! Kenji was very honorable, and he used his rank to protect *Ninang* Gloria and me. I have never seen him or known of him being associated with the atrocities during the occupation. If anything, he tried to stop it," Imelda said as she fiercely defended Kenji.

Adele sat up and exclaimed, "This is a mess! And you! You were a comfort woman?! Who knows about this? Why did you keep it a secret?"

That remark irritated Imelda, and it was very evident on her face. "Because I did not want this!" she answered forcefully.

Adele was taken aback and have realized how bad she had reacted to her mom's revelation. "I am sorry mom. You just caught me by surprise. This doesn't change anything between us. I will always love you, mom."

She walks over to Imelda and puts her arms around her. Imelda starts to cry as she embraces Adele. Soon, Adele too was crying. They held on to each other for some time.

Finally, Adele asked, "What are you going to do now? What about dad?"

Imelda wiped off the tears on her face and said, "So much has happened these past weeks. I did not like what I have become after the occupation. I know now that I have to change. These past weeks have changed me. And yet, I am still finding myself."

Imelda took a seat and pulled a couple of tissues from the box to wipe off her tears. "I am going on a trip. Not sure where and how long.

"*Ninang* Gloria was correct. I lost something a long time ago, and I need to find it. I need to find myself. I am taking a chance that it is not too late to discover what it is that I genuinely want to be. All I know is that this is not me, and I have to get on my chosen path."

Adele took a seat next to Imelda and she put her arm around her waist. "Mom, do what you have to do. Everything will be alright," Adele assured her gently.

Imelda faced Adele and took her hand. She said, "When something so horrid happens to you, you want to run and hide, but I am done hiding. I am still here and I want to live."

"And you will mom," Adele reassured her by gently rubbing Imelda's back.

"I just need to sort things out for myself. But I am not running away to hide again," Imelda stated sincerely.

Imelda stood up and walked towards the glass window again. She looked out to the courtyard outside, trying to find an anchor. Imelda felt like she needed space and yet had to hold on. Trying to rein in all her emotions.

"Living with a secret is a death sentence," she said. "It is a poison that slowly kills one's spirit. The cost is tremendous and harms not just oneself but others too. I could not and would not share my secret then because my fear was great. But I am done with all that."

Adele stood by her mother's side and took her left hand and firmly squeezed it. "Mom, you do what is best for you. You deserve to live. You have so much life still to live. Go and seize it. We will be here for you. I will always be your *favorite*," Adele said as she briefly smiled when she alluded to her pet name.

Imelda smiled at Adele, "Silly, you are my only child. Of course, you are my favorite. I live vicariously through you."

Adele gently hugged her mother and lovingly whispered, "That's the thing, Ma. It is time you lived the life you want to live and not through me but for yourself."

Imelda tightly embraced Adele and then she pulled back. She cupped Adele's face with her hands and struggled to say a word.

Mother and daughter looked at each other, exchanging nothing but knowing stares. They embraced again and Imelda declared, with a hint of triumph in her voice, "My story is not finished."

FIN

GLOSSARY

Anak – Tagalog word for child.

Aray – Tagalog word for ouch.

Barong Tagalog - An embroidered long-sleeved formal shirt for men and a national dress of the Philippines.

Bayong – Tagalog word for a basket usually made out of dried leaves native to the Philippines.

Calamansi – Philippine lime.

Danna - A powerful, wealthy man that pays for all the expenses of the geisha. To become a geisha requires a lot of time and money. The danna would pay and take care of the geisha throughout her life, therefore, it was a high social status to become a danna. It showed that they had enough money to be a patron of a geisha.

Dirty Kitchen – The kitchen where the Filipinos do most of their cooking, usually at the back of the house.

Ensaymada - A type of Filipino brioche. Soft, sweet dough pastry covered with butter and sugar then topped with lots of grated cheese.

Geisha – A female Japanese professional entertainer who attends to guests during meals, banquets, and other occasions. They are trained in various traditional Japanese arts, such as dance and music, as well as in the art of communication. Their role is to make guests feel at ease with conversation, drinking games, and dance performances.

Heredera – Tagalog word heiress.

Hija – Spanish endearment for daughter.

Hukbalahap – Acronym for "Hukbong Bayan Laban sa Hapon" (English: The Nation's Army Against The Japanese) An anti-Japanese Army formed by the peasant farmers of Central Luzon during the war. They are popularly known as the "Huks."

Ingat – Endearing Tagalog word for careful meaning "to take care."

Itay – Tagalog word for father.

Kalesa – Tagalog for a horse-drawn carriage used in the Philippines.

Kanpai – Japanese word for cheers in a drinking toast

Kariton – Tagalog for a farmer's working cart normally pulled by a water buffalo or a horse.

Lambanog – A traditional Filipino distilled palm liquor made from coconut or nipa palm sap. It is derived from the juice of a young coconut and aged for at least 48 hours.

Makapili - Makabayan Katipunan Ng Mga Bayani or Alliance of Philippine Patriots was a militant group formed in the Philippines during World War II to give military aid to Japan. Organized by Benigno

Ramos and Artemio Ricarte, they were born out of José P. Laurel's refusal to conscript Filipinos for Japan.

Mamasan – A Japanese woman in a position of authority, especially the madam of a geisha tea house. In the story, "Mamasan" was used as a proper noun like a name.

Mataray – Tagalog word used to describe women who answer you back in a sharp, snappy way.

Mutya ng Lipa – Tagalog word for gem or jewel and often refers to a young adolescent girl muse. In this case, Mutya ng Lipa means Muse of Lipa or Queen of Lipa.

Merienda – Tagalog word for snacks.

Nanay – Tagalog word for mother.

Ninang – Tagalog word for godmother.

Oiran - The highest-ranking sex workers in Japan.

Papag – A Tagalog term for a "low bamboo bed."

Peineta – A Spanish word for a large decorative hair comb.

Sala – Tagalog word for living room.

Sampaguita – National flower of the Philippines. Sweet-scented tropical flower

Señorita - A title or form of address that refers to a Spanish-speaking unmarried woman, equivalent to "Miss."

Silong – Tagalog word for basement.

Suplada - Tagalog adjective used to describe girls and women who are not friendly.

Tabo – Tagalog word for "dipper."

Talahib – Tall grass seen on empty lots with white flowers like giant feathers. Scientific name: Saccharum spontaneum.

Tio – Spanish term for uncle.

"Wala kang hiya." – Tagalog for the phrase "you have no shame"

Walis Tingting – Tagalog word for a broom made from the thin midribs of palm leaves.

Yaya - Filipino version of the European governess. They are servants in the homes of Filipino families belonging to the upper class of society.

ON THE COVER

The front book cover is a rendering of Imelda in the 1980s by Angeli Clarisse Lata with Yolanda Ortega Stern standing in as the model. The illustration depicts the older Imelda guarding her secret fiercely that one has to literally tear it off her to reveal the beaten and sexually assaulted younger Imelda.

The artist, **Angeli Clarisse Lata,** is an up-and-coming artist and visual storyteller from the Bay Area, California. Her artwork reflects a variety of influences from various schools of painting: from the expressionist to surreal; from abstract to street art. She considers the works of Frida Kahlo, Jackson Pollack, Henri Matisse, Paul Gauguin, Margaret Keane, Andy Warhol, Takashi Murakami, Miss Van, Robert Bowen, and Alex Pardee— to name a few, as her major influences. A history and culture enthusiast, her work highlights the complexities of gender, sex, human rights, and racial/ethnic diversity through her use of brilliant and contrasting colors as well as focus on portraiture.

Her work has been exhibited at the San Francisco Mint, East Bay Community Center in Oakland, CA, and at the San Francisco Philippine Consulate. She has also partnered with local coffee shops in the area to showcase her art, notably at the Barrelista in Martinez, California. On the web, her paintings can be found at @angelisartstudio.

She is currently working on an initiative in support of the Black Lives Matter movement through her project Banners for Change. Her group is producing artworks used as banners that the people carry during protests. The movement aims to humanize victims of systemic oppression and honor their families who are organizing this fight. Similarly, her work on "Imelda's Secret" has allowed her to illustrate the atrocities of war and depict women in their fight to be seen and recognized by a system that has ignored them for much too long.

Her work has inspired many and has been used as a voice for those who have historically held less to no power in society – to spotlight the stories that have been glossed over by historians in the past.

Angeli's art showcases the nuances and the diversity of the human identity and experiences. It exposes the truth that exists in life and functions as a mirror before the world, showcasing the ugly and the beautiful from the female perspective.

The model, **Yolanda Ortega Stern,** is a Berkeley Educator (retired) and is the current chairman of the One World Institute (USA) and OWIC Philippines – both are private not-for-profit foundations engaged in philanthropy for peace projects. The foundations were founded in 2000 with her late spouse, Dr. Thomas K. Stern with initial support from the Berkeley Family Practice Medical Group, Berkeley-based medical facilities owned and co-managed by Ms. Stern. The foundations are primarily focused on health and education through reading programs, humanitarian missions and various livelihood projects.

Known as a "Daughter of Mindanao," Ms. Stern has many years of experience in conflict resolution, human rights issues, immigration policies and entrepreneurship. Ms. Stern was appointed Hon. Ambassador of California in 1994 for work bridging trade and commerce between the USA and Asia. She spearheaded the Reacquisition Act that led to the Dual Citizenship Law in the Philippines and became the first dual citizen. She served as senior adviser to key organizations with intimate knowledge of the history of the armed struggle in Mindanao, Philippines and the history of Filipino and Latin immigration to the US. She is also the author of "Sex and The Wild Pearl," the definitive resource book on mollusks of the Sulu Seas that produce natural pearls.

The book back cover is a mixed media mosaic glass art entitled "Iluminati 3" by Maria Isabel Lopez. It's a metaphorical representation of Imelda after her transformation. The women known as "comfort women" were practically "stoned" because of the ignorance, prejudices, misguided taboos, and society's inequitable application of justice. This is Imelda rising. The stones now represent the jewels on her back. She is now empowered and ready to walk away from all the pains of the past, bare and naked, wearing only the truth as her armor.

The artist, **Maria Isabel Lopez,** is an award-winning Filipino actress and a Fine Arts graduate of the University of the Philippines. She's a former Secretary of the National Commission for Culture & Arts-Committee on Visual Arts from 2011 to 2013.

She describes "Iluminati 3" as: "The female body is in itself a work of art though not necessarily perfect. Individual fragments, imperfect and broken, were combined in such a way to reveal a rich tapestry for the senses. A wide variety of materials were used in Iluminati 3, including natural and manmade stones, foraged and found items such as horseshoe crab carcass, abalone, and sea glass. This was done by contrasting elements of light and shadow, shape and texture in the fluid lines of the subject matter. The element of light was reflected in the use of brilliant colors that are magical; a glorification of the human flesh."

Her earlier mosaic pieces show a desire to experiment with found objects – river pebbles, sand mortar, shells, and natural stones to create highly textured compositions.

Her background in fashion design brought her this fascination of the female form. Her decades-long career as an actress allowed her to use her body as an acting tool. This brought creativity, spontaneity and balance through her other art form – the language of mosaic.

AUTHOR'S BIOGRAPHY

Liza Gino grew up in a small town in the Philippines to a large family with no shortage of uncles, aunts, cousins, and grandparents. Growing up, her extended family gave her the experience and tradition that is steeped in the Catholic faith. Her upbringing afforded her the understanding of family dynamics, its hierarchy, and due order. Filipino values can be complicated and chastity is a premium. Having to put chastity over family can be challenging, thus making the plight of Filipina comfort women arduous.

There was no shortage of stories about the Japanese occupation from her family and friends. Narratives of what one had to endure, especially for women to survive, impressed upon her. She was shocked to realize that very few were aware of the saga of the comfort women. It was the associated shame of the act that women decided to bury the truth. These stories provoked her to write this novel. Liza believed that everyone should be aware of the plight of the comfort women and help

LIZA GINO
Author

them reveal the truth; to set aside taboos, ignorance, and even personal pride in order to help and support all women who were victims of sexual tyranny.

As a graduate of the University of the Philippines, it awakened her radicalism and activism. She wanted to be an agent of change, especially for women. She believed that by having the mindset changed, women could demand to be respected and cherished. She proposed the idea that they deserve a place under the sun to thrive and be contributing members to humanity.

Imelda's Secret is Liza's way to imbue a message of change and inspire advocacy. When these women were abused, their fundamental rights to life, freedom, health, and peace of mind were forcibly taken from them as well. The author hopes that this novel would have the exposure that would bring acknowledgement, validation and respect on a global scale of the stories of the comfort women. The fictional stories of Gloria and Imelda will hopefully give prominence to the true saga of the real victims of war so that their sacrifices and the raping of their lives are no longer a buried secret in history.

SYNOPSIS

Imelda's Secret is based on several true accounts from family and friends about the Japanese occupation of the Philippines written into one storyline. This novel is not another war story but a story about redemption, advocacy, and strength of the comfort women. Their plight continues way after the war and demands attention and action.

The novel is about two *heredera* cousins, Imelda and Gloria, who survived World War II. Forty years after the war, they are now living in San Francisco, California, dealing with the trauma of their experiences during the war. Gloria has revealed that she was a comfort woman, whereas Imelda kept it a secret.

Gloria's disclosure hurt her and her sons deeply. Together with Imelda's daughter, Adele, they started to gather other comfort women and advocate for them. Gloria is now dying and is imploring Imelda to tell her story as a comfort woman and continue her fight because it is in the interest of all women to safeguard against sexual tyranny.

Imelda lost a lot during the war and saw how Gloria was ostracized instead of being supported. She kept her secret to protect herself and her daughter. Adele did not know about Imelda's secret. Fearful that her secret will change everything, she refused to speak of it. Gloria's impending death forced Imelda to face the truth. There are other reasons that are compelling Imelda to speak up. One unforeseen element is the appearance of a Japanese Colonel at her door in San Francisco.

Imelda's Secret is life changing. Her nondisclosure was meant to protect her and her family and, yet, the truth cannot stay hidden forever. Changes are coming and Imelda has to brace for it.